KINSMEN

A "Nameless Detective" Novella

Bill Pronzini

KINSMEN

A "Nameless Detective" Novella

Bill Pronzini

CEMETERY DANCE PUBLICATIONS

Baltimore
❖ 2012 ❖

FIRST EDITION
ISBN: 978-1-58767-266-8
Cemetery Dance Publications Edition 2012

Kinsmen
Copyright © 1993 Bill Pronzini
Dust jacket illustration by Glen Orbik
Dust jacket design by Gail Cross
Typesetting and book design by Robert Morrish

Cemetery Dance Publications
132-B Industry Lane, Unit 7
Forest Hill, MD 21050
Email: info@cemeterydance.com
www.cemeterydance.com

Dedication

For Marcia

1.

The northeastern corner of California, where it joins Oregon on the north and Nevada on the east, is different from other parts of the state. Not geographically; there are sparsely populated, mountainous regions spread throughout California. What sets Modoc and Lassen counties apart, first, is their remoteness. There are no large or even small cities within a radius of hundreds of miles, no major highways; it takes hours of hard driving to get there from San Francisco or Reno or one of the Oregon cities. The area has its share of scenic attractions: Modoc National Forest, South Warner Wilderness Area, Lassen National Forest, dozens of little bodies of water with quaint names like Horse Lake and Moon Lake and Big Sage Reservoir. It also has some of the best hunting and fishing anywhere on the west coast. But the effort required to get there, and a dearth of the usual tourist amenities, keeps visitors to a relative minimum even in the summer and fall.

A hefty percentage of the residents prefer it that way. And that is the other thing that sets the Corner apart: the attitudes and mind-set of its people. They like their back water status and their privacy; they tolerate hunters, fishermen, skiers, tourists, but unlike the inhabitants of other rural areas they don't actively cultivate outsiders. And some of them are rural-minded to the point of clannishness and hostility.

The largest town up that way is Susanville, population 7,000, in lower Lassen County. Alturas, near the Oregon border in Modoc County, has half as many residents. The rest of the towns in the two counties are either villages or wide places along highways 395, 299, and 139—places most native Californians have never even heard of. Newell, Fort Bidwell, Lake City, Cedarville, Davis Creek, Likely, Madeline, Termo, Ravendale. And Creekside. Creekside, California, population 112.

Until this Wednesday morning I was one of the natives who had never heard of Creekside. Now, at four-thirty in the afternoon, after nearly six long hours of driving, the last hundred miles over roads still snow-hemmed even though it was early May, here I was in the town itself. It wasn't much by anybody's standards. Wide place not far off Highway 395, about equidistant between Susanville and Alturas, rimmed by mountains and closely edged on all sides by pine and fir forests. Two-block main drag, winter-potholed, and some short side streets that climbed a hillside and gave access to a scattering of old frame houses and newer log structures squatting among the trees. The business establishments were few and mostly on the east side of Main. Creekside General Store. Trilby's Hardware and Electric, "We Sell Natural Gas." Modoc Cafe. Eagle's Roost Bar and Card Room, "Dancing Every Saturday Nite." Maxe's Service and Garage. And at the far end, near the second of two access roads that took you to and from 395—Northern Comfort Cabins, Off-Season Rates, Vacancy.

I turned in past the rustic Northern Comfort sign. The motel was not particularly inviting, even to a weary traveler who had been on the road for more than six hours. A dozen small pine board cabins, set in twin rows of six that faced each other across an unpaved courtyard like old soldiers on a rundown parade ground. The office building was bigger but just as old and not as straight-standing: seedy drill instructor fronting his motley troops. Behind the last of the cabins, where the forest edged in close, a stream ran fast and frothy—the creek, probably, that had given the hamlet its name.

There were no other cars on the property to keep mine company, except for an old Buick with its chrome snout peeking out from behind the office. The whole place had the look of desertion, even with lights on inside the office and smoke twisting out of its chimney.

I got out into a fast-gathering twilight. Cold up here; you could still taste winter in the air. The rush-and-hiss of the stream running was audible even at a distance of a hundred yards, swollen as it was with snow run-off. It made me think of trout, fat rainbow trout, and the feel of my old rod with its Daiwa reel, and the way a mountain stream tugs and swirls around your legs. And of how long it had been since I'd gotten away for a few days of fishing. Hell, for a few days of any kind of vacation. If things were better between Eberhardt and me…

Wishful thinking. Things weren't good at all between us—so strained, in fact, that not only was a fishing trip out of the question, I was worried that maybe our partnership and our long-standing friendship were in jeopardy. Problems related to his aborted wedding plans in April were one reason—maybe the main one, maybe not. He'd changed in the past year or so, become distant and broody. And I had no idea why.

I flexed some driving kinks out of my shoulders and back, went inside the motel office. Small, rustic, dingy. On one wall was a framed, hand-stitched motto that said *Praise God;* on another was a brass sculpture of a cross and a pair of praying hands. There was nobody behind the narrow counter at the back, not until I bellied up to it. Then a door opened and a tall, cadaverous party came through. He moved in a slow, painful shuffle, as if he had back problems. He was about my age, late fifties, with a beak of a nose and loose skin in folds under his chin and ears and hair that poked up in thin wispy patches around his scalp. He put me in mind of a molting turkey.

"Help you?"

"I'd like a cabin."

"Sure thing. Just tonight or longer?"

"Probably just tonight."

"Got your pick," he said. "Close to the road or farther back. Cabins in back are real quiet."

"That sounds good."

"Give you number Twelve."

He put a key and a registration card on my side of the countertop. I laid a credit card and the photograph of Allison Shay on his side. As soon as he saw the photo, his face closed up. He looked at it for a long time, with his chin tucked down in its nest of wattles. When his head finally came up, his eyes told me nothing at all.

He said, "Police officer?"

"Private investigator."

"Girl's family hire you or what?"

"Her mother."

"I already told the county sheriff everything I know. Which ain't nothing much."

"Mind telling me, Mr.—?"

"Bartholomew," grudgingly.

"Mr. Bartholomew."

"They checked in, they spent the night, they left next morning. I never even seen him. Girl came in for the room. Otherwise—"

"Otherwise what?"

He shook his head.

"Late afternoon when they checked in, wasn't it?" I asked. "Last Friday afternoon, about this time?"

"That's right."

"Which cabin did you give them?"

"Eleven. In back, opposite the one I give you. But they didn't leave nothing behind. My wife does the cleaning up; she'd of found it if they had."

"What time did they check out on Saturday?"

"Didn't check out. Just left the key in the cabin."

"Did you see them leave?"

"No," Bartholomew said. "I told you, I never seen the two of 'em together. Or him at all."

"She didn't put his name on the registration card?"

"No. Just hers."

"Didn't mention it? Even his first name?"

"Just said her boyfriend. Some other time I wouldn't have rented to her."

"Why?"

"Why did I? It's slow time and we need the money."

"No, I mean why wouldn't you have rented to her?"

"Wasn't married. Sharing a bed out of wedlock is a sin."

"Uh-huh. Any idea what time they left here on Saturday?"

He shrugged. "Art Maxe, down at the garage, says he had their car ready at nine and that's when they picked it up."

"When the girl checked in," I said, "did she happen to mention what route they planned to take, side trips, anything like that?"

Headshake this time. "All she said was her and her boyfriend been having trouble with their car and they got it into Maxe's Garage just before it quit on them. And wasn't it lucky they was this close to a town when it happened."

While we'd been talking I had filled out the registration card. As I slid it over to him I said, "Mind if I take Cabin Eleven instead of Twelve?"

"What for? I told you, there's nothing in there that'll tell you where them kids went."

"I'd still like Eleven. If you don't mind."

"Why should I mind," he said, and gave me the key to Cabin Eleven. I smiled at him before I went out. He didn't smile back.

2.

As with Creekside itself, there wasn't much to the cabin. Small, bare, barely functional—a wooden cell designed for those who came here to the Corner expecting to rough it. Four coarse-pine walls, unadorned except for a framed hunting print and, hanging low and off-center over the bed, a sepia-toned picture of Christ wearing a crown of thorns. Dresser, nightstand, bedframe all of scarred pine. New, board-hard mattress covered by a cheap quilt. TV set that had been manufactured about the time of the first Super Bowl. The bathroom was a cubicle with an ancient toilet and a zinc-floored shower. In the old days one of the slang terms for toilet was "growler"; this one reminded me of why. It made noises like an angry pit bull when you flushed it.

Cold in there, too. The only heating appliance was a space heater; I switched that on before I sat on the hard mattress. From outside I could hear the muted rush of the stream. It had an oddly lonesome sound.

I took out the photo again, studied it. Allison Shay. Candid shot, in color, about six months old; just her, full-body, taken reasonably close so that her features were clearly defined. Slender, almost slight. Light blonde hair, worn long with a center part. Snub nose, small smiling mouth, round eyes that her mother said were blue-gray. Pretty. Intelligent; she had maintained a high B average throughout her three years at the University of Oregon. Studying architecture. Not a common field for a woman and more power to her. Activist, on and off campus: women's issues, liberal politics, environmental causes.

I knew a fair amount about Allison Shay, all right, but virtually nothing about the boyfriend—not even his name. Marian Shay had never met him, hadn't even known her daughter was involved with anyone until Allison called a week ago and said she was taking a few days off from school and driving down to the Bay Area "with a friend." She wouldn't name the friend, just said it was someone she wanted her mother to meet. She'd sounded bubbly—Marian Shay's word— and that, coupled with the "few days off from school," had led Mrs. Shay to believe the friend was male, Allison was serious about him, and the purpose of the trip was to show him off. That was the way Allison was, Mrs. Shay had told me: mischievous, inclined to be mysterious when it suited her, prone to sudden decisions and deep commitments.

Allison and her companion had left Eugene on Thursday, in her old MG; but instead of taking the direct route, straight down Highway 5, they'd veered over into the Corner to "do a little exploring" on the way down. Allison's explanation when she'd called home again on Friday night, from here in Creekside, to tell her mother about the car breaking down. They were due into Orinda, where Marian Shay lived, on Saturday evening and Allison said she thought they could still make it "if the man at the garage gets the car fixed and it doesn't break down again." She'd still sounded happy and excited; no hint of any problem other than the one with the MG.

That was the last Marian Shay had heard from or about her daughter. No sign of Allison on Saturday or on Sunday; a Sunday phone call to the motel here had gotten her the same information that Bartholomew had just given me. When she still hadn't had word on Monday morning Mrs. Shay had notified the authorities. But the police wouldn't list Allison as officially missing until Tuesday, when the mandatory seventy-two hours had elapsed, because of her age and the circumstances of her driving trip south. You could understand that from their point of view; kids in love were liable to do all sorts of crazy things on a whim, with little or no consideration for their parents, and the cops had been burned too many times by false alarms. From Marian Shay's point of view, the delay was exasperating. She'd called the house in Eugene where her daughter was living and checked with her roommates; Allison hadn't returned and none of the roommates could tell her anything about the new boyfriend. The manager of the bookshop where Allison worked part-time also had nothing to tell her. Nor did Allison's best friend in Orinda, who usually shared confidences with her; she hadn't heard from Allison in weeks.

Monday dragged on through Tuesday. The preliminary police investigation failed to turn up a lead to Allison's whereabouts, or as yet the identity of the boyfriend. This morning, frantic and frustrated, Marian Shay had come to me. And caught me with no pressing business and in the right frame of mind, thanks to the problems with Eberhardt, for a case that would take me away from the city for a few days.

I repocketed the photograph, sat looking around the cold bare room that Allison Shay had shared with her lover last Friday night. Assume the boyfriend was a college student, too, someone of Allison's age. How would they have felt, spending the night here? Viewed it as part of an adventure, maybe, as kids will. Backwoods interlude; snuggle up in this monastic cell, make love and their own heat, make the best of it. Or maybe it hadn't been that innocent or idyllic. Maybe they'd had a fight of some kind, and the next day it had kindled even hotter, and then…what? He abandoned her somewhere in the backcountry, and took her car and drove himself back to Oregon? Not likely, but possible. Hell, *anything* was possible. The car broke down again and this time they weren't lucky enough to be close to a town and they'd managed to get themselves lost on foot. Or they'd had an accident. Or they'd made the foolish mistake of picking up the wrong kind of hitchhiker. Or—worst-case scenario—the boyfriend hadn't been what he'd seemed to Allison, was in fact some kind of psycho in sheep's clothing. Nowadays, in this kinder, gentler society we live in, that sort of thing happens too damned often.

Five days now, and not a whisper.

Long past the inconsiderate-kids stage; long past the silly and the harmless. Whatever had happened to Allison Shay, it felt like something bad. Her mother thought so, too; it had been in Marian Shay's pale face, in the faint stunned expression in her eyes, in the damp marks her restless fingers had left on her suede purse. Neither of us had put the fear into words, but the words had been there between us—and they were in my mind again now.

Wherever she is, is she still alive?

3.

In the cluttered, droplit maw of his garage I found Art Maxe with his head and upper body underneath the raised hood of a Jeep Cherokee, working the accelerator linkage to race the engine. The blonde kid manning the pumps out front had told me this was where Maxe was. I walked up alongside the Jeep and waited until he quit jazzing the engine.

"Art Maxe?"

He said, "Yeah?" without shifting position.

I told him who I was and why I was there. That brought him out of the Jeep's shell. He was big and shaggy and dirty, like a bear that had been rolling around in a pile of oily refuse. There were oil streaks on his unshaven cheeks, a glob of grease caught in his unkempt black hair; his overalls looked as though they had never been washed and his hands were black-spotted with the kind of imbedded grime even industrial-strength soap can never quite get out. He gave me a long steady look out of squinty eyes that held both wariness and suspicion.

"I already talked to the county cops," he said.

"Then you won't mind talking to me. I'm trying to do the same job they are— find a couple of missing kids."

He shrugged. "You ask me, they took a side road somewheres and that car of theirs busted down again. Lot of wilderness around here, lot of places to get lost."

"You don't think much of the car?"

"Piece of junk. Just about ready for the dismantlers."

"What made it quit running last Friday?"

"Fuel pump went out. I didn't have one in stock, not for one of those foreign jobs; had to call down to Susanville. They couldn't get it up here until early Saturday."

"And you had the car ready for them when?"

"About nine," Maxe said. "I warned 'em, though. Half a dozen other things were ready to go on that baby. Don't push it too hard, I said. She just laughed, the girl. Allison?"

"Allison."

"Yeah. Kids that age, everything's a big joke."

"Who was driving when they left, him or her?"

"She was."

"They say which direction they were going?"

"Not to me. Out to the highway and then who knows?"

"Which of them paid for the repairs?"

"She did. In advance."

"How did they seem together that morning?"

"Seem?"

"Toward each other. Were they getting along all right?"

"Better than all right," Maxe said. "Just like the day before—kidding around, laughing. Holding hands. Christ, even kissing on each other." He shook his head and made a spitting mouth, as if he thought public displays of affection were obscene.

"Either of them mention his name? The boyfriend's?"

"Not that I remember."

"First name, even a pet name?"

"No."

"How old would you say he was?"

"Her age, about."

"Describe him."

"Shit, I'm no good at that…"

"Didn't the authorities ask you for a description?"

Shrug. "I couldn't tell them much either."

"How tall was he?"

"Not too tall. Average."

"Six feet? Shorter?"

"Six feet, about."

"Weight?"

"One-seventy, one-eighty maybe."

"In good shape?"

"Well, he filled out a sweater pretty good."

"What about his hair? Short, long?"

"Short. Real short."

"What color?"

"Well now what color you think?"

"I'm asking you, Mr. Maxe."

"Black."

"Any memorable feature? Mouth, eyes, nose?"

"No."

"Scars, moles?"

"No."

"Anything at all unusual about him?"

"…I dunno what you mean."

"Did he limp, talk oddly—like that."

"No. He was just a…just a kid, that's all."

"How was he dressed?"

"Blue sweater, Levi's, them running shoes."

"Both days?"

"Yeah."

"And the girl?"

"Same, only her sweater was green."

"Was anybody else here when they came on Saturday morning? Anybody they might have talked to?"

"No."

"Kid out on the pumps?"

"No, just me. Johnny don't come in until ten, Saturdays." Maxe made a waggly gesture with the wrench he was holding. "I got work to do," he said. "How about you letting me get back to it, huh?"

"All right."

"Questions like you been asking ain't gonna find 'em anyway. They got lost, like I said. They'll walk out under their own steam or the county sheriff's pilots'll spot 'em from the air. Otherwise…" Another shrug. "Bones," he said.

4.

There were two people in the Creekside General Store when I walked in: behind the counter, a heavyset woman in a plaid lumberman's shirt, and in front of it, a male customer wearing a stocking cap over long hair tied in a ponytail. It was a dark, crowded place with a creosote-soaked wood floor; narrow aisles and tall shelves. In addition to the usual merchandise, there was a back section stocked with old clothing and miscellany, a sign above it reading "Thrift Corner."

I loitered near the door, waiting for the counter transaction to be consummated. On the wall was a corkboard to which were attached dozens of business cards, flyers, and scraps of hand-written notepaper. People wanting goods and services; people selling same. Cordwood, yardwork and hauling, and babysitting were the dominant subjects. One of the flyers was something else again—something nasty. It had been printed by an outfit called the Christian National Emancipation League, run by a "Grand Pastor" named Richard Artemus Chaffee—one of those white supremacist outfits that preach hate instead of love under the guise of religion. It wasn't local, though; the address and telephone number were downstate in Modesto. Put here by a traveling League member, probably: saturation recruitment drive that reached even into backwaters like this. I quit reading it when the stocking-capped customer came away from the counter with his groceries. But I would have quit anyway about then; credos such as "dedicated to purifying America of race-mixing and mongrelism, and to the emancipation of the white seed and the rise and rebirth of God's true Chosen People" make me want to puke.

The ponytailed guy was in his late forties, and the length of his hair and beard, the out-of-date ragbag clothing he wore, marked him as a child of the sixties—a former hippie for whom time had stopped somewhere around 1967. He didn't want anything to do with me, maybe because to him I represented the establishment in my suit and tie. He shook his head when I tried to talk to him, refused to look at Allison Shay's photograph, and pushed past me and out through the door. Peace and love to you too, brother, I thought.

The heavyset woman was even less cooperative. She glowered at me as I approached and said before I got to her, "Don't bother showing it to me neither. I can't help you."

"I just want to know—"

"Never saw those kids, neither one."

"At least take a look at the girl's picture—"

"Can't help you, mister. Didn't you hear me tell you that? This is a store, not a hangout; buy something or leave."

I left. On the way out I tore down the Christian National Emancipation League's flyer and crumpled it and threw it into a sidewalk trash can. That made me feel a little better.

Trilby's Hardware and Electric was closed, so I moved on to the Modoc Cafe. Too-hot box, its trapped air thick and miasmic with the odors of frying meat, grease, coffee, cigarettes, and human effluvium. Booths along the side walls, a few tables in the middle, serving counter and kitchen at the rear. The patrons totaled six, all in the left-hand booths; it was early yet, not much past five-thirty. I sat in one of the right-hand booths and waited for the lone waitress to work her way around to me.

Fortyish, tired, with a polite outer layer over a hard inner core of cynicism and quiet desperation: it went with the job in places like this, or maybe it was the job that made women like her the way they were. Her name was Lena, according to one of those little oblong badges on the pocket of her uniform. She set a well-thumbed menu in front of me, asked if I wanted coffee.

I said I did and then held up Allison Shay's photo. She glanced at it, took a longer look at me. The cynicism was in her eyes now, along with a certain wariness, but none of the politeness seemed to have chipped away; even her faint professional smile remained intact.

She said, "And who would you be?"

"Private investigator."

"No kidding." She wasn't impressed, or even particularly interested—at least not in me or my origins.

"You recognize the girl?"

"If you mean was she in here, yeah, she was. Only place to eat in town."

"Last Friday night?"

"As I remember."

"With a male companion?"

"Him, too."

"You wait on them?"

"I'm the only waitress, most nights."

"Did she happen to mention his name?"

"Once that I heard. It was noisy but I think she said Rob."

"Rob, not Bob?"

"Rob."

"Anything about his appearance or actions strike you as unusual?"

"Not really. Good-looking kid, not too dark."

"What nationality, would you say?"

Her smile dipped wryly. "American," she said.

"How did they act together?"

"Like they were alone in a bedroom."

"Couldn't keep their hands off each other?"

"Right. In a place like this, in the middle of the Friday dinner rush…stupid. Very stupid."

"Why stupid?"

"Calling attention to themselves like that."

"Yes?"

"These are the mountains, mister, not the big city." Lena poked a stray lock of brown hair back over one ear. "Coffee, you said. Cream, sugar?"

"Just black."

She went away and I opened the menu. I hadn't eaten since breakfast, and then only juice and a bowl of Grape Nuts, and I was hungry. The closest thing to low-fat, low-cholesterol food served here was pot roast and I was not in the mood for pot roast, particularly not when I saw the listing for chicken-fried steak in country gravy.

I have had a small insatiable lust for chicken-fried steak all my life. Back in the days when I was overweight and eating all the wrong things, I would order it every time I saw it on a menu—ongoing search for the ultimate chicken-fried steak, blue-collar equivalent of the white-collar pursuit for a perfect martini. I had kept my weight down for well over two years now, after shedding forty pounds under the grimmest circumstances imaginable three winters ago; retrained myself to eat and drink in healthy moderation, and to maintain a regular exercise program. I hadn't had chicken-fried steak in all that time and I was overdue. One little indulgence wouldn't hurt me. One little rationalization, either.

Lena came back with my coffee and I ordered the chicken-fried steak. Then I asked her, "The girl and her boyfriend have much to say to you while they were here?"

"No. They were too wrapped up in each other for chit-chat."

"Just placed their orders and that was all?"

"Pretty much."

"What were they talking to each other about?"

"I didn't pay much attention."

"Travel plans? Anything like that?"

"I just said I didn't pay much attention."

"Okay. They talk to anyone else, one of the other customers?"

"…No."

"Why the hesitation?"

Lena looked down at her pad, moving her lips in an over-and-under motion as if she were holding a debate with herself. Pretty soon she said, "Not in here. Afterward, out in front."

"Who was it they talked to then?"

"I don't know. I saw them through the window, just for a few seconds, and it was dark out there."

"One person or more?"

"Two. Two men, I think."

"But you don't have any idea who they were?"

"You think I'm lying?"

"No, I don't think you're lying. How long did they talk?"

"Couldn't have been long," Lena said. "Next time I glanced through the window, they were gone. All of them."

"What time was that?"

"End of the dinner rush…about seven-thirty."

"You see them again that night?"

"No."

"Saturday morning, before they left town?"

"I wasn't here Saturday morning. I don't work the breakfast shift."

"Who does?"

"Andrea. Ask her tomorrow morning."

"I'll do that."

"Mashed potatoes or French fries with your steak?"

"Mashed potatoes."

Her smile quirked again. "Good choice," she said.

It wasn't. It turned out to be a lousy choice all around. The mashed potatoes managed to be lumpy and runny at the same time, the country gravy was mostly white sauce with neither Tabasco nor black pepper, and the patty-sized "steak" was a mass of gristle coated with corn meal instead of flour. If the perfect chicken-fried steak was a ten, this one barely made it past zero. No wonder Lena's smile had been wry.

So the ultimate chicken-fried steak was still out there somewhere. Maybe. Or maybe, like the perfect martini—or for that matter, like Diogenes' honest man— it didn't really exist except as an illusionary ideal. Not that it mattered either way. The important thing was the quest itself, the search for perfection in an imperfect world.

5.

The Eagle's Roost was like every backcountry tavern I had ever set foot in, down to the heads and horns of dead animals displayed on the walls and the jukebox packed with sob-and-throb country tunes. At one end was a tiny dance floor and bandstand, and beyond that, through an archway, was the card room. Both the bar and the card room were moderately crowded, to the point where nobody paid any attention to me. Walk into an unfamiliar place like this when only a few patrons are present and they'll all stop what they're doing to look you over, wonder who you are and why you've wandered onto their turf. Walk into a crowded place like this and it's just the opposite: you're not an individual, just another cell in the crowd body. That's the way it is with lynch mobs, too. And one of the reasons strangers can incite men who would not even speak to them under other circumstances.

I found an empty stool at the far end of the bar. The bartender was fat, about as jolly as a slug on a dry rock and just as slow; it took him nearly five minutes to work himself my way. I used the time to flash Allison Shay's photo at the rough-dressed men on either side. None of them wanted anything to do with it or with me; I was interrupting their happy hour and their penetrating discussions about deer hunting, baseball, and whether or not dynamite was the best way to uproot a stubborn tree stump.

When the bartender finally got around to me I tried the photo on him. He wasn't interested either. "Can't you see I'm busy?"

"Just take a look," I said. "It's the girl who disappeared last week—"

"I don't know nothing about that. You drinking or not?"

"Not right now."

"Then don't take up that stool, huh?"

He shuffled off, and I thought: Bad idea, trying to work cooperation out of a crowd of backwoods boozers. Let it go for now. Come back later, maybe, when the crowd thins out. Or, hell, maybe not.

I swung off the stool and started out, and somebody at one of the tables reached up to flick at my coat sleeve. Art Maxe. He was slouched in a chair with a bottle of Bud in one hand and a cancer stick in the other. Across from him sat a tall, blonde scarecrow of a man with bright eyes and cratered cheeks. That one seemed to think I was worth staring at. He wasn't quite smiling but I had the impression that there was laughter lurking somewhere inside him.

Maxe said, "You having any luck?"

"Not so far."

"Don't know why you keep bothering. They got lost somewheres, like I told you."

"Could be. But I get paid to bother."

"You a good detective, are you?"

"Some people think so."

"In the city, might be. Not up here."

"No? Why not?"

"These mountains, they got secrets nobody can find out. Not even one of us natives."

The laughter quit lurking inside the skinny guy and came dribbling out in a thin, high-pitched giggle. I didn't like hearing it; it made me think of Richard Widmark in *Kiss of Death,* just before he pushed the old lady in the wheelchair down a flight of stairs.

"What's funny?" I asked him.

"Nothing," he said. "Nothing's funny."

"Don't mind Gene," Maxe said. He tapped his temple. "Everybody says old Gene Ballard ain't all there and I guess they're right. How about it, Gene? You playing with a full deck or not?"

"Couple of aces missing," Ballard said, "but the joker's still there. Yes, sir, the *joker's* still there."

His shrill giggle followed me out, lingered in my ears like a slow-dying echo even after I shut the door. Early spring night in the mountains: sharp-cold, with a high wind running clouds down a moonless sky. House and building lights shone hard, brittle, without much warmth. The air was thin in my lungs but heavy with the rich scent of pine and fir. It was a good night for walking—the Northern Comfort was so close I hadn't bothered with the car; the kind of night, in the kind of mountain setting, that ought to lift your spirits, invigorate you. Not me, though, not tonight. Not in Creekside.

I didn't much care for this town. Maybe it was because I was an intruder and had been made to feel like one. Maybe it was the people I'd encountered—Bartholomew, Maxe, Gene Ballard, the fat bartender and the aging hippie and the woman in the general store. Maybe it was the lousy chicken-fried steak. Or maybe there wasn't any specific reason, just the fact that some places, regardless of size or location, generate negative energy that affects certain people. Different places for different individuals. Anyone who is at all sensitive to his surroundings has experienced this at least once, a distaste and an unease that won't go away while you're there.

I would be glad to leave here in the morning. The earlier the better.

6.

The space heater had warmed Cabin Eleven considerably, though I could still feel the night chill seeping in through the walls. There was a telephone on the nightstand, with a little card scotch-taped to the base that told you all long-distance calls had to go through the office. It was a woman who picked up in there—Mrs. Bartholomew, no doubt. I gave her Marian Shay's number and she said she'd get it for me. She sounded stiff and grudging, as if I were asking her to do something that went against her grain.

Marian Shay answered on the first ring, and the mixture of eagerness and dread in her voice told me before she did that she'd had no word from the police. My report snuffed out the eagerness, flattened the dread under a dull weariness.

"The boy's name may be Rob," I said. "R-o-b. Is that familiar to you?"

"…No. No, I'm sure Allison never mentioned that name."

"Doesn't look like there's anything else for us here," I said. "In the morning I think I'll try another approach—drive up to Eugene, see if I can identify Rob. His family or friends may know something."

"All right," she said, "whatever you think best. But call me tomorrow, midday? Please? Even if you don't have anything to tell me. I need…" She didn't finish the sentence.

"I know," I said. "I'll call you."

We said quick hushed goodbyes, like furtive lovers, and I rang off feeling depressed. In my mind was an image of her—early forties, blonde like her daughter, on the heavy side—sitting tensed by the phone, waiting, alone. She was several years divorced, not seeing anyone right now, and by her own admission a private person who had few friends…all alone with her pain and her dread.

I got Bartholomew's wife on the line again and gave her Kerry's number. I hadn't told Kerry I was going away from the city, and talking to her always cheered me—two good reasons to call. But not as good as the third reason, which is that I am so hooked on Kerry Wade I need to see her or at least hear her voice as often as a heroin addict needs to ride the white horse.

She was surprised when I told her where I was, and a little wistful when I said I might be away for three or four days. But the timing, she said, was probably right because she expected to be pretty busy herself the rest of the week.

"How come?" I asked.

"New account." She was a senior copywriter at Bates and Carpenter, San Francisco's best (to hear her tell it) small ad agency. "Luau Fashions, of Honolulu, owned by an idiot named Arthur Dykstra."

"Why an idiot?"

"He's one of those people who become successful in spite of themselves. Started on a shoestring five years ago and now he's the biggest manufacturer of men's and women's Hawaiian shirts in the islands. Not the cheap variety; the fancy art deco aloha shirt made out of silk crepe de chine that costs a hundred and fifty dollars apiece. Now he's expanding his operations to the mainland—that's why he hired us."

"Sounds like a relatively easy sell to me," I said. "What's the problem?"

"The slogan he's come up with for his ad campaign. I can't talk him out of it, and if I have to use it it's going to drive me crazy. And him out of business inside a year."

"What is it?"

"'Shirt Happens,'" she said.

I burst out laughing.

"It's not funny. My God, can you believe the man is serious? A pun based on an obscenity to sell fancy Hawaiian shirts to *families?* Dykstra thinks people will find it 'charming.' I've told him over and over he's wrong, Doug Bates has told him over and over, but he just won't listen. The man is an *idiot...*"

I let her rant. She seemed to need a sympathetic ear tonight and I did not feel much like talking about the Allison Shay disappearance or my experiences in Creekside. And just listening to her lifted my spirits—the old tonic working its usual miracle cure.

Lord, I love that woman. Would have married her by now if she weren't so dead-set against the concept. Not of a union with me—of the institution itself. She'd had one bad marriage and it had soured her forever, or so she claimed. I had quit proposing to her, but I hadn't quit on the idea of making her my wife; my campaign these days was much more subtle and clever, and I kept telling myself it was having an effect. She *was* weakening; it was just a matter of time.

The irony of this wasn't lost on me: sex-role reversal, the tough male the one doing the frantic scheming to snare a mate. But it didn't matter. I was shameless when it came to Kerry Wade. Hell, I'd have had her child if I wasn't already past the age of male menopause...

7.

Andrea, the day-shift waitress at the Modoc Cafe, had the same inner core of cynicism and quiet desperation as Lena, but none of the pleasant veneer. She said, sourly, that she had never laid eyes on Allison Shay or her boyfriend—and when she set my coffee down she did it hard enough to slosh some over into the saucer. No surprise, I thought, that the missing kids hadn't stopped for breakfast on Saturday morning. They had probably wanted out of Creekside as badly as I did.

I showed Allison's photo to some of the other early-morning customers, without results. It was just seven-thirty when I left the cafe. The town had a more friendly aspect at this hour, with few citizens to clutter up its natural beauty. Mist lay among the trees at the higher elevations, had put a sheen of wetness on the streets and sidewalks. It was going to be a nice day, at least so far as the weather went.

So—north to Oregon and Eugene? The other option was to take Highway 395 south, canvass the four or five other little towns between here and Susanville, and then do the same in Susanville itself; but the Lassen County Sheriff's Department would already have done that, or be in the process of doing it, and the odds-against were long in any case. I liked the idea of going to Eugene better, even though it meant another long drive. Once I knew who Rob was, it might give me a more definite direction to explore, instead of having to run around scattergun as I was.

Except for an occasional logging truck, I had the northbound side of the highway pretty much to myself. I was in Alturas, the Modoc County seat, before nine o'clock. I stopped at the sheriff's office there and spoke to a deputy named Collins. He had nothing to tell me. He'd been in contact with the Lassen sheriff's department earlier this morning, he said, and so far they hadn't turned up any leads either.

"Those kids could have disappeared anywhere between Creekside and the Bay Area," Collins said. "Doesn't have to be in one of our counties."

"I know it."

"Could even be they made it to within a few miles of home before something happened. Down there in your own backyard."

I knew that, too. Too well. If that was the case, the chances of my finding Allison and Rob would be a lot slimmer. The Bay Area is a much bigger haystack.

From Alturas I took Highway 299 east to Canby and then 139 North into Oregon. I stopped in Klamath Falls for gas, and from a public phone I called Marian Shay. Painful two minutes: we had nothing to tell each other, nothing to trade except more entreaties for more empty reassurances.

The drive from Klamath Falls to Eugene took a little better than three hours. The weather up here wasn't half as good as it had been in California. Oregon is a wet state—

the University of Oregon's sports teams are not known as the Ducks for frivolous reasons—and wet was what I encountered: drizzles above Roseburg, steadily increasing rain as I rolled northward. By the time I reached Eugene I was in the midst of a downpour.

Like a lot of Oregon, Eugene is a green place. That's your first impression and the one that lingers after you've gone away. It lies between the foothills of the Cascade and Coast mountain ranges, and along the Willamette River—the center of a rich agricultural and lumbering region. I'd spent some time there on a case years ago; it had struck me then as a pleasant town to live in despite the weather. I had the same feeling now.

The house Allison Shay shared with four other female U of O students was on Hilyard just off 22nd, within walking distance of the campus. Neighborhood of older homes, built in the twenties and thirties, many of them now converted into off-campus student housing. Wraparound front

porch on Allison's, gingerbread still cling-
ing tenaciously to its facade. There were no
cars in front or in the driveway—nobody
home to answer the bell.

It was a short drive from Hilyard to the
city center. The Unicorn Bookstore, where
Allison worked part-time, was on Willamette. I had to park a block away and I
was damp and dripping when I walked in.
Big place, new and used stock of both text-
books and general trade books, packed with
students and fussy-looking, untidily dressed
older people who might have been teachers
or welfare clients. (These days, I thought,
is there much economic difference between
the two?) The store's manager was in his
early twenties, bespectacled and so chinless
it looked as though a bite had been taken
out of the lower half of his face. His name
was Peverell.

"I can't understand it," he said. "Allison
is such a responsible person." He sounded
fussy and much older than his years, like
one of his senior customers in training.

Bill Pronzini

"Something must have happened to her, don't you think?"

"Such as?"

"Oh, I wouldn't want to speculate."

"Neither would I. Did Allison tell you she was going home for a few days?"

"Yes. She works Saturdays and she asked for last Saturday off. It was short notice but we try to be flexible."

"Uh-huh. She give a reason for the sudden trip home?"

"No," Peverell said. "But it seemed important to her. She was…excited, I guess you could say."

"Did you know she was making the trip with a male friend?"

"Not until her mother told me."

"His name is Rob. You know anyone by that name?"

"Rob? No, I don't think so."

"You're sure she never mentioned him?"

"She's not one to talk about her private life."

"So you don't know any of her male friends?"

"Just Gary Oster."

"Who's he?"

"A guy she was dating."

"Dating when?"

"Until recently. I don't know for how long."

"How recently?"

"I'm not sure. He used to pick her up after work sometimes. I hadn't seen him in a while and I mentioned it to Allison a couple of weeks ago and she said she wasn't seeing him anymore."

"Why not?"

"She didn't say."

"And you didn't ask?"

"It wasn't any of my business."

"What about this Gary Oster? Student at the university?"

"Yes."

"Where does he live?"

"I can't tell you that. I barely know him."

"Know anybody who does know him?"

Peverell shook his head. "Just Allison," he said.

Down the block from the Unicorn was a coffee shop. I went in there and drank two cups of decaf and read through today's issue of the Eugene *Register-Guard*. There was nothing in it about the disappearance. At five o'clock I loaded myself into the car again and drove back through the steady rain to Hilyard Street.

A car was now parked in the driveway alongside the big old house, a lemon-yellow Volkswagen bug. The young woman it belonged to turned out to be Karyn Standish ("that's Karyn with a 'y'," she informed me), one of Allison's roommates. Short and compact in Levi's and a bulky knit sweater, she led me into an empty front room where a stereo system was giving out with classical music, something moderately dour in keeping with the weather outside. She sat in a loose-hipped sprawl in one of several narrow chairs; I squeezed my hams into another one facing her.

"It's really weird, you know?" she said. "I mean, you read about things like this, people just disappearing without a trace, but

when it happens to one of your friends…"
She hugged herself. "Weird and scary."

I nodded. "Ms. Standish, you know
that Allison went to California with a male
friend—"

"Actually, I didn't. Not until her mom
told Jeanne—that's another roommate —
on the phone Sunday night."

"She must have mentioned she was going away."

"The trip, sure. Not that she was going
with somebody."

"His name is Rob."

"Really?" She sat up straighter "Rob
what?"

"No last name yet. I thought you might
be able to supply one."

"Damn," she said. "I don't know any
guy named Rob. Are you sure that's his
name?"

"Pretty sure."

"Not Bob? I know a couple of Bobs."

"I was told it's Rob. Allison is close-
mouthed about her male friends, is she?
Even with her roommates?"

"Oh, she talks about her love life sometimes, when she's in the right mood. Who doesn't?"

I don't, I thought. "But not about Rob."

"No."

"How about Gary Oster?"

"Gary? Sure. They were close for a while."

"What happened?"

She shrugged. "They broke up."

"When?"

"Six or seven weeks ago."

"Why, do you know?"

"Al wouldn't say. But I think she's the one who ended it."

"Because she'd met Rob, maybe?"

"Well, it must be. She's been going out a lot the past month. We all thought it was just casual stuff, you know, to get over Gary, but it could have been just one guy, somebody new and special."

"So new and special she wasn't ready to talk about him yet."

"Right. I guess she wanted to keep him all to herself for a while."

"How well do you know Gary Oster?" I asked her.

Karyn Standish showed me small, sharp teeth in a smile that was half ingenuous and half wicked. "Not as well as I'd like to. He's a hunk. I still think Al was nuts for letting him go."

"How did he take the breakup? Hard?"

"I think so. He seemed pretty bitter."

"Bitter enough to hold a grudge, do something foolish?"

"…You mean to Al?"

"Or to Rob. Or to both of them."

"Uh-uh, no way. Not Gary."

"He bother Allison in any way after the breakup?"

"What do you mean, bother her?"

"Keep calling her, keep hanging around."

"No, nothing like that."

"Would she have told you if he was giving her a hard time?"

"Probably. Anyhow, we'd have known even if she hadn't. There's only one phone here, and one of us would have seen him if he'd been hanging around."

"Can you tell me where Oster lives?"

"One of the frat houses, I think. I'm not sure."

"Does he have a job?"

"I don't think so. His dad's a doctor. He's not in pre-med, though. Business major."

"Is there any place I might find him, somewhere he goes regularly in the evening?"

"Well, there's Porky's."

"What's that?"

"Pizza parlor over on Pearl. It's a Ducks hangout…you know, U of O students. I don't go much myself—I can't do pizza and beer very often with my figure—but when I do, Gary's usually there."

8.

Porky's was big, noisy, garishly lit, and crowded. Half the customers looked to be college students; the other half, at this early hour, were a mix of adults and pre-teens, most of whom seemed to be regulars who were trying their damnedest to live up to the name of the place. There was enough excess body tallow distributed throughout to start a candle factory.

Gary Oster wasn't in attendance, not yet. One of the half-dozen college kids manning the pizza ovens and beer spigots knew Oster and said he came in most nights after seven-thirty. I considered having my dinner there while I waited and rejected the idea immediately. Last night's chicken-fried disaster was enough high-cholesterol food for the week.

I drove along Pearl until I found a quiet-looking restaurant with only a few cars in its parking lot. Roast chicken and a dinner salad gave the digestive juices something to work on, and allowed me to use up an hour in relative peace. It was a few minutes past eight when I reentered Porky's.

The parlor was even noisier and more crowded now, though most of the excess tallow had been replaced by college students who were slimmer and more energetic, if no less hungry and thirsty. Gary Oster was one of them; the employee who knew him pointed him out. He was sitting alone at a two-person table in the rear, a half-full pitcher of dark beer at one elbow, brooding into a mug that he had clenched in both hands. He was a broad-shouldered kid, chunky without being fat, dark-complected, with dark shaggy hair. He didn't know I was there until I slid into the chair across from him; then his head came up, jerkily. His eyes were dark, too, under rat's-nest brows, and bright with a combination of hurt and smoldering anger.

"Gary Oster?" I said.

"Who the hell're you?"

"I'd like to talk to you about—"

"Go away. I don't want to talk."

"Not even about Allison Shay?"

He made another jerky movement, this one bowing his body forward so that his chin was almost resting on the pitcher of beer. He narrowed his eyes at me. "What do you know about Al?"

"I know she's missing."

"Yeah," he said. "You a cop?"

"Private investigator, working for Allison's mother." I told him my name. I tried to show my license at the same time but he didn't want to look at it.

"What happened to her?" he asked grimly. "You find out anything yet?"

"Not yet."

He took a long swallow from his mug, refilled it from the pitcher with hands that were not quite steady. He wasn't drunk, at least not yet. The shaking was a product of something else—fear, self-pity, a scattershot anger that had no real focus.

"Five days," he said. "She's been missing five days and I just heard about it this morning."

"Who told you?"

"Angie Walters. One of her roommates."

"Did you know she'd gone to California?"

"How would I know? I haven't talked to her in weeks, not since she…" He broke off into a short brooding silence. Ended that by banging the flat of his hand on the table, hard enough to swivel heads in our direction. "Shit," he said. "Why'd she have to take up with him? Why *him?*"

"Who? Rob?"

"If he's responsible," Oster said, "if he did anything to hurt Al, I'll kill him. I swear to God I'll kill him."

"Rob?" I said again. "Is that who you're talking about?"

"Who the hell else?"

"Rob what? What's his last name?"

"Compton. Rob fucking Compton."

About time, I thought. "You know him, then."

"Oh yeah, I know him."

"Tell me about him."

"Tell you what?"

"Where he lives, for starters."

"Over on Eighteenth. Married students' housing."

"Compton's married?"

"No. Singles live there, too." Oster made a derisive nasal sound, like a flatulence in his sinuses. "Special privileges. Yeah."

"He live alone or with roommates?"

"One roommate. Cottages aren't big enough for more than two people. Perkins, Ken Perkins. I went over there this morning, after I talked to Angie. Waste of time."

"Perkins didn't know anything?"

"No. Said he didn't anyway."

"What's Rob Compton like?"

"Smart. Straight A's, Dean's List…that's the big reason Al turned on to him. Full of big-crank ideas."

"Such as?"

"Change the world. All that liberal bullshit."

I had nothing to say to that.

"I tried to tell her," Oster said. "But she wouldn't listen."

"Tell her what?"

"What she was getting into. She said I was prejudiced. I'm not prejudiced, god-damn it. I love her, I want to marry her, I don't want to see her hurt."

"Wait a minute," I said. "Back up a little. Why would she accuse you of being prejudiced?"

"Why do you think?"

"I'm asking you. I don't know anything about Rob Compton or Allison's relation-ship with him. I'm blundering around in the dark here."

"Dark," Oster said bitterly. "Yeah, right."

"Gary…"

"Rob Compton's black," he said.

9.

The married-students housing facilities on Eighteenth off Patterson had a military look, like Army dormitories—probably because they had been built during World War II. Impermanent housing that became permanent as the university's enrollment grew steadily larger. Little cottages sewn together in long rows separated by blacktop lanes with narrow berms and speed bumps every few yards. Each had a peaked roof, tiny yard, tiny stoop; some sported picket fences; most seemed to have an outside array of bicycles, tricycles, strollers, kids' toys, and/or yapping dogs.

It took me a while to find the cottage shared by Rob Compton and Ken Perkins; I had to ask directions twice. Its uncurtained front window was lighted, the outspill showing a relatively well-tended yard.

The car parked in front was a ten-year-old green Datsun.

Ken Perkins turned out to be lean, studious-looking, with one of those pillbox hairdos that have replaced Afros among younger blacks. When I identified and explained myself he seemed eager to cooperate. Inside were two rooms and a kitchenette, all of them college-student untidy: books and papers strewn over every available surface. Perkins cleared a raggedy Goodwill chair of a sociology text and a library copy of a book by Chester Himes and invited me to sit down.

"I don't understand it," he said. "It was just a trip down to the Bay Area to see their people. A big deal to them but no *big* deal. You know?"

I nodded. "Rob's from the Bay Area too?"

"El Cerrito. We both are."

"Did he know Allison down there?"

"No. They met here."

"Just recently?"

"Couple of semesters ago. They had the same psych class."

"But it was just recently that they became involved."

"About six weeks ago. They were both on the Student Council and they got to be friends and then they fell, hard."

"How hard? How serious is their relationship?"

"Pretty serious," Perkins said. "That's why they decided to go home, see their people—get them over the shock in person."

"Then what? Marriage?"

"That's the plan."

"How soon?"

"Not until next year, after they both graduate."

"With or without the approval of their families?"

"Yes. Al thought her mother would understand…well, he wasn't so sure about his folks. His dad's old-fashioned." Perkins grinned sardonically. "Maybe the right word is bigoted. The races shouldn't mix, separate but equal, all that."

"Do the Comptons know about the disappearance?"

"I called his dad as soon as I got the word from that asshole Oster. He was pretty upset."

"No word from or about Rob in the past week?"

"None. Rob hadn't even told his folks he was coming home."

"Did you tell his father about Allison?"

"Her being white? No. Just her name and that they left here together, were driving down as a surprise."

"Would you mind giving me the Comptons' telephone number? And their address, if you have it?"

"Anything you want, if it'll help."

"I could use a photo of Rob, too," I said.

"There ought to be one around here somewhere."

He went into the bedroom and poked around in there for three or four minutes. In one of the adjacent cottages a baby was squawling, loud enough so that the kid might have been in the room with me.

Must be fun trying to study in quarters like these. Oster had said Rob Compton was "privileged" to have gotten this housing as a minority single student. Some privilege.

Perkins came back with a 3 x 5 snapshot and a piece of notepaper with the address and telephone number of Rob Compton's parents. "Photo's of the two of us," he said. "But it's the only one I could find."

It was a color snap, probably taken on the university campus, Perkins and Compton with their arms across each other's shoulders, mugging a little for the camera. Compton was a nice-looking kid, large-boned and large-framed, all of his meat evenly distributed and without any trimming of fat. Hair cropped close to his skull. Long-fingered hands. Infectious smile.

"This will do fine," I said. I put it with the photo of Allison in my jacket pocket. "You don't like Gary Oster much, I take it."

"Why do you say that?"

"Well, you called him an asshole."

"I did, didn't I." His mouth quirked wryly. "That's what he is, all right."

"Any way in particular?"

"All ways. What Al saw in him is be-yond me. She's a nice lady, smart, percep-tive. I guess maybe he was her blind spot."

"We all have 'em."

"Rob's the one who opened her eyes," Perkins said. "Made her see that Oster's a racist, among other things. She wouldn't have anything more to do with him after the blowoff."

"What blowoff is that?"

"When she told him she was quitting him for Rob. He threw a fit. Called Rob names, called her names—ugly scene."

"Were you there?"

"No. Rob told me about it."

"Did Oster threaten either of them?"

"Not in so many words. You think he had something to do with the disappear-ance?"

"Do you?"

He thought about it. "Hard to say. I don't know him that well. Don't want to know him at all. But if he was up to some-thing nasty, why wait six weeks? And why

not do it here, in Eugene, instead of following them into California?"

Good questions. I said as much.

"Lot of crazy people running around
these days," Perkins said. "People you
know, people you don't know. Just can't tell
by looking, or when or where you might
run into one. But I guess you know that, in
your business."

"Unfortunately."

"If Rob and Al…" He didn't finish it.
And I didn't finish it for him.

10.

I found a motel off Highway 99 not far from the campus. In my room, first thing, I called Marian Shay, even though it was getting on toward ten o'clock. She'd been waiting and waiting to hear from me, she said. And from the tremor in her voice I knew even before she spoke again that she also had news. Bigger news than mine.

"They found Allison's car," she said.

"Where?"

"In Eureka."

"Eureka?"

"Parked in a public lot downtown. It... the police said it had been there at least three days. There were parking tickets... that's how they knew."

"What was in it?"

"Nothing to suggest...well, you know."

Foul play was what she meant. "Clues to where they might be?"

"The police said no."

"Her luggage? His?"

"Both suitcases were locked inside. There wasn't anything in the man's to identify him."

"That problem's solved," I said. "I've found out who he is."

I told her about Rob Compton—everything I'd learned except for the fact that he was black. Marian Shay would probably have taken the news all right; Ken Perkins had told me Allison expected her mother to approve of her relationship with Compton. But I did not want to give her anything more to deal with tonight. She had enough with the finding of Allison's abandoned MG.

When I was done she said, "Do you think..." and seemed to choke on the rest of the words. She cleared her throat and started over, haltingly. "Do you think he... Rob Compton...I mean, that he..."

"I know what you mean," I said gently. "No. From the people I talked to here, he's a good kid in every way."

It didn't reassure her much. "Why would they go to Eureka?" she said. "I don't understand that, when they were way over in Modoc County."

There was only one way it made sense to me, with the superficial knowledge I had, and I did not want to get into that with Marian Shay, either. I asked her, "Did you talk to an officer from the Eureka police?"

"No. To the man from the Orinda police, the one who took the missing persons report."

"What's his name?"

"Donaldson. Frank Donaldson."

"When did he contact you with the Eureka news?"

"This afternoon. Two-thirty or so."

Call him in the morning, I thought, see if there's anything he held back to spare Mrs. Shay's feelings.

She said, "Will you go to Eureka tomorrow?"

"I don't know yet."

"But if that was the last place Allison…"

"Whatever I do tomorrow, I'll keep you informed."

She drew a shuddery breath. "I don't know how much more of this I can stand. I've been eating Valium like candy."

What can you say? More empty reassurances? I muttered a lame suggestion that she try to get some rest and broke the connection.

While I was sitting there with the phone, I wondered if I ought to call Rob Compton's parents in El Cerrito. No, not tonight. Chances were, they didn't know anything more than Marian Shay about the disappearance; and it was late and I wasn't up to long explanations tonight anyway, particularly not if Compton's father was against interracial relationships and didn't know Allison was white. Maybe I'd call him tomorrow. Or better yet, let Frank Donaldson be the one to initiate contact.

All the driving the past two days had fatigued me, but it was a physical tiredness only. My mind was in one of those hyperactive states where you know damned well you're going to have trouble putting it to rest. No point in going to bed yet. Instead I went into the bathroom and ran a tubful of hot water and got in it to soak and think.

Eureka. I didn't like that, not at all; it put a new and disturbing slant on things. Eureka was on the coast, the largest town in the northern part of the state, some 250 miles due west of Modoc and Lassen counties. It didn't add up that after the MG had already broken down once, and a mechanic had warned Allison of other potential problems, that she and Compton would take a reverse course from Creekside all the way over to Eureka, much of the distance over rough wilderness roads. Sure, college kids were prone to spur-of-the-moment decisions and risk-taking adventures, and it was possible they'd had enough of the mountains and determined to swing across to the coast, drive down scenic Highway 1 to the Bay Area. But under the circumstances, and given what I'd learned about Allison and Rob and their plans, it damned well wasn't likely.

The only other explanation was that they *hadn't* gone to Eureka; that a third party had driven the MG there. Red herring: abandon the car a long way from the real disappearance point to throw the authorities off the track.

Foul play, in that event. Worst-case scenario.

I ran more hot water into the tub. Gary Oster? Followed them down from Eugene, confronted them at some point after they'd left Creekside, committed an act of violent revenge? That would be stretching credibility pretty thin. Same was true for somebody else they'd known up here. There was just no sense in anyone following them several hundred miles into the California mountains and then waiting around overnight before attacking them.

Stranger or strangers, then. Allison and Rob in the wrong place at the wrong time in conflict with the wrong people.

Modoc or Lassen counties? It didn't have to be. After they left Creekside they could have run into trouble, as deputy Collins had said, anywhere in a several-hundred-mile radius stretching all the way south to the Bay Area. But now there was the Eureka factor. If the MG *had* been abandoned as a red herring, it was probable Eureka had been picked because it was far—but not too far—away and because it was the nearest good-sized town, one where an abandoned vehicle would not go unnoticed for long. Large towns were much more numerous once you got out of the mountains to the south.

Modoc and Lassen counties were still the best bet.

And to narrow the focus even more, there was Creekside, the last place Allison and Rob had been seen. The unfriendly little hamlet of Creekside.

I kept thinking about the fact that Rob Compton was a black man. Nobody in Creekside had volunteered that information, to the authorities or to me, and neither the sheriff's deputies nor I had asked the right questions to bring it out. Now that I knew, certain things people had said to me yesterday—some subtle, some not so subtle— took on significance.

Bartholomew, at the Northern Comfort: *I never seen him. Girl came in for the room. Otherwise—*

Art Maxe: *Holding hands. Christ, even kissing on each other.* And the spitting mouth he'd made as he said those words.

Lena, at the Modoc Cafe: *Good-looking kid, not too dark… Couldn't keep their hands off each other. In a place like this, in the middle of the Friday night dinner rush…stupid. Very stupid. Calling attention to themselves like that. These are the mountains, mister, not the big city.*

Was that the key to the disappearance, a black man traveling those mountains with a white woman?

Some kind of Creekside conspiracy—of silence if not of action?

I remembered other things, too, now. Maxe saying in the Eagle's Roost: *These mountains, they got secrets nobody can find out.* The ugly high-pitched giggle of the scarecrow named Gene Ballard. Lena telling me she'd seen Allison and Rob talking to two men after they'd left the cafe on Friday night. And the flyer that had been posted in the Creekside General Store—the flyer from an outfit called the Christian National Emancipation League that was "dedicated to purifying America of race-mixing and mongrelism, and to the emancipation of the white seed and the rise and rebirth of God's true Chosen People…"

11.

I was up early again in the morning, on the road by seven-thirty. No rain today; broken clouds and cold winds. I drove straight down Highway 5 and reached Medford before ten. On the southern outskirts I found a service station that had a booth with a working telephone, and called the Orinda police department.

Frank Donaldson was in, but I had more to tell him than he had to tell me. He'd been in touch with the Eureka police again a short while ago, he said; they had no leads from the MG or the kids' luggage to who had abandoned the car or why. I explained what I'd learned in Eugene, and gave him the address and telephone number of Rob's parents in El Cerrito. He thought they and Marian Shay ought to be told the whole truth and volunteered to do the telling. I was more than willing to leave the chore in his hands.

One more call. In better times, it would have been to Eberhardt, even though I knew he was working long hours on an insurance-fraud case; agency partners turn to each other when they need help, or ought to. As things stood, with the strain between us, I made the call to Joe DeFalco at the San Francisco *Chronicle* instead. DeFalco was an old poker buddy who had been with the paper twenty-odd years; I figured he wouldn't mind doing me a favor as long as it didn't require too much effort. Joe is high-energy only when it suits him, which is when there's something involved that will benefit Joe DeFalco.

"What is it you need?" he asked.

"Specifics on an outfit called the Christian National Emancipation League. Name familiar to you?"

"Vaguely. Some kind of racist group."

"Right. Based in Modesto, of all places. Address on Milltown Road. The head of it—'grand pastor,' he calls himself—is

somebody named Chaffee, Richard Artemus Chaffee."

"Shouldn't be too difficult. Anything
else?"

"Whether or not there's a connection
between this League and a little town in
Modoc County called Creekside. Or between the League and that part of the state."

"Uh-huh. So what're you working on
that you're mixed up with racists?"

"Missing persons case," I said. "Couple
of college kids who disappeared last week.
And I hope to Christ it has nothing to do
with racists."

"Can of worms if it does?"

"Big can of worms. The missing girl is
white and the missing boy is black."

"What do you think, foul play by this
Christian National Emancipation League?"

"Maybe. Or by somebody connected
with them."

"Want me to call you when I have the
poop?"

"Better if I call you. You be in later today?"

"In and out," DeFalco said. "Mostly in after three."

"After three, then."

The rain clouds that had soaked Oregon yesterday had blown south into California. I picked up the stragglers just after I crossed the state line at Tule Lake, and it was raining hard enough coming through the Modoc National Forest to force my speed down to an average of forty. It was past one o'clock when I rolled into Alturas.

I stopped again at the sheriff's office, to see if they or the Lassen County authorities had turned up anything. They hadn't. As with Frank Donaldson, I told the deputy named Collins about Rob Compton's race and gave him the address and telephone number of Rob's parents. He didn't seem to think there was anything in the racial angle. I wished I agreed with him.

At two-fifteen I was back in Creekside. Dismal little place under a wet gray sky: empty streets, the collection of frame and log buildings looking huddled and oddly insubstantial, as if they were sets built for a Hollywood location shoot. You had the feeling that the lights behind their windows were skillfully placed reflector lamps, and that any door you opened would lead you not into a room but into more wet gray daylight.

I parked in front of the Modoc Cafe, went inside. No customers; the only person in the big room was Andrea, the day-shift waitress, sitting in one of the booths with a cup of coffee and a cigarette. She didn't seem pleased to see me again. Nobody here, I thought, was going to be pleased to see me again. I asked her what time Lena came on; she said four o'clock. Then she said, "What do you want with Lena?"

"Few more questions, that's all."

"Questions about what?"

I smiled at her.

She said, "Why don't you leave us alone, huh? Nobody here knows anything about what happened to those kids."

"If you say so, Andrea."

There was a little silence, while she waited for me to go away. I didn't go away. Pretty soon she said, "Now what do you want?"

"A bowl of soup and a cup of coffee."

"What kind of soup?"

"What's the house specialty?"

"Cream of road kill," she said.

"…Is that supposed to be funny?"

"Nothing is funny around here. We got hearty beef and chicken noodle, take your pick."

I picked chicken noodle. Another bad choice. It was lukewarm and the fat eyes floating on top kept me from eating most of it; I don't like to be stared at by my food. I didn't call Andrea when I was done. Instead I looked up the prices on the menu and left the money on the table. Exact amount, no tip.

* * *

The same heavyset woman was in charge of the Creekside General Store, doing something in one of the cramped aisles. We were alone together after I walked in. I paused by the door to scan the corkboard on the wall. The flyer I'd torn down on Wednesday had not been replaced.

When she recognized me, the woman's eyes took on a refrigerated look. A rat in one of the produce bins would have gotten a warmer reception. "You again," she said.

"Me again."

"I don't know any more than I did the other day, so there's no use you bothering me. Buy something or get out."

"How about a membership in the Christian National Emancipation League?"

"The what?"

"There was a flyer on the bulletin board the last time I was here. Put out by the Christian National Emancipation League. Mind telling me who put it up there?"

"How should I know? People put all kinds of crap on that board. What do you think it's there for?"

"But you never saw it, right?"

"No, I never saw it."

"Don't know what this League is all about."

"Mister," she said, "I don't know nothing about nothing."

But her eyes had flicked away from mine, to roam the close-packed shelves. She knew, all right. She knew about the Christian National Emancipation League and she knew who had put that particular piece of crap on her bulletin board.

12.

At the Northern Comfort Cabins the court-yard was rain-puddled and empty. I angled my car in close to the office, with the driver's side nearest the entrance so I would have to take only a couple of steps to get inside. It was raining as hard now as it had been in Eugene yesterday, thick wind-driven lancets out of gray-black clouds that seemed to hang just a few hundred feet above the village. The low overcast made me think of Joe Btfsplk, the character in "Lil Abner" who had a cloud of gloom and doom hanging over him everywhere he went. If any single impression of Creekside and its citizens stayed with me, this would be it. A real-life Dogpatch with an entire population of Joe Btfsplks.

At first I thought the office was untenanted, but as I approached the counter a female head covered with stringy, gray-streaked hair came into view behind and below it. The face under the hair was round and puffy and sagging, as if all the flesh were slowly rotting away beneath the skin. One of the reasons, or maybe the main reason, was gin: she had a glass of it in one hand and the air in the too-warm enclosure was ripe with the juniper-berry smell. She was sitting in an old cushioned armchair with her feet up on a stool; to one side of her, next to the door into the rear living quarters, was a portable TV with its screen dark. She might have been anywhere between forty and sixty, round-bodied, fat-ankled, wearing a shapeless muu-muu of the type that had gone out of style twenty years ago.

I leaned on the counter. "Mrs. Bartholomew?"

"That's me." Raspy voice, unfuzzied by the gin. She was the kind of heavy drinker, I thought, who would sound completely lucid right up to the moment she passed out. "Who're you?"

I told her. Something changed in her eyes—a darkening, a shifting, almost a retreating. Up came the glass; down went the rest of the gin in it, a good two fingers. She didn't even blink.

"Well?" she said. "Why'd you come back?"

"Just doing my job. Your husband around?"

"No. Went up to Alturas. You want a cabin, I suppose."

"If you've got a vacancy."

Either the irony escaped her or she chose to ignore it. "Got nothing but vacancies, this time of year. You care which one?"

"Eleven."

She didn't comment on that. Nor did she get up out of her chair. "Seventy-five a night," she said. "In advance."

"Price was fifty-five two days ago."

"New rates." Her eyes challenged me to argue.

I didn't give her the satisfaction. There was a stack of registration cards on the counter; I took one and filled it out. Mrs. Bartholomew watched me with her gin-bright eyes, but still she made no move to stand up.

I said, "You want me to fill out the credit card slip, too?"

"I'll do that. You can reach the key yourself."

I reached the key off a rack at one end. She moved then, in a series of slow pushings and liftings that were almost like a parody of the ritual movements of Aikido or Tai Chi. I waited until she was on her feet before I said, "What can you tell me about Allison Shay and Rob Compton?"

"Same as Ed told you. Nothing." One of her hands gobbled up my MasterCard; it was the fastest I'd seen her do anything except suck down the gin.

"You did see them while they were here?"

"I saw them."

"Talk to either one?"

"No."

"What did you think about them staying here together? Black man, white woman?"

Her mouth thinned down. "The Lord's business, not mine."

"So it didn't bother you."

"I got nothing against niggers," she said.

"Your husband feel the same way?"

"He does. What're you harping on that for? What's that have to do with them two wandering off someplace?"

"Maybe they didn't wander off someplace," I said.

"No? What'd they do, then?"

"Got into some trouble, maybe. Right here in Creekside."

"What trouble?"

"With a couple of local men who aren't good, tolerant Christians like you and your husband. That's one possibility."

"Nonsense," she said. "Wasn't no trouble the night they were here, nor the morning they left town."

"They have any visitors that night?"

"Here? Who'd visit them here?"

"Meaning nobody did?"

"Meaning I don't spy on my guests."

"Allison called her mother," I said. "She and Rob make any other calls Friday or Saturday?"

"No."

She finished scratching numbers on the credit card slip; slapped it and my Master-Card down in front of me. I signed the slip, pocketed my copy and the card.

"Nice talking to you, Mrs. Bartholomew."

"You think so?" she said.

I smiled at her, the kind of smile with lots of teeth and no humor, and went to the door and then stopped and turned and said, "One more thing. Who do I talk to in Creekside about the League?"

She was on her way through the door back there, probably going after more gin; the words halted her, stiffened her back. She half-turned before she said, "The what?"

"The Christian National Emancipation League. Who do I talk to about it?"

She said, "I don't know what you're talking about," and took the lie with her out of sight.

13.

The blonde kid, Johnny, was alone on the premises of Maxe's Garage, huddled up in the tiny office with a space heater between him and the cold rain outside. He wasn't any more glad to see me than Mrs. Bartholomew. He had been nervous in my presence on Wednesday; today he was fidgety as a baby with a loaded diaper.

"Mr. Maxe ain't here," he said.

"That's all right. I want to talk to you, too."

"Me? Nothing I can tell you."

"Sure about that?"

He wouldn't make eye contact. "I'm sure."

"What are you afraid of, Johnny?"

"Afraid? Nothing…"

"Your boss?"

"No, I told you, nothing."

"Where can I find him?"

"I don't know. He left about one o'clock."

"Went home, maybe?"

"I don't know."

"Was he alone or with somebody?"

"…Gene Ballard."

"Uh-huh. They're good friends, right?"

"I guess."

"What's he do for a living? Ballard."

"He…yardwork, hauling…you know, that kind of thing."

The kid's tongue kept making skittery movements along his upper lip. There was sweat on him now. Gene Ballard was one of the things he was afraid of; I could see it in his eyes.

"You get along with Ballard all right?"

"Sure I do. I get along with everybody. Why?"

"Kind of a funny guy, isn't he?"

"Funny?"

"Weird. That laugh of his…gives you the willies."

"Yeah," he said.

"Like he's a little crazy. You think he is?"

"I…I wouldn't know."

"How does he feel about blacks?"

"…What?"

"Black people. He doesn't like them, does he?"

"Geez, how should I know how he—"

"That's why he joined the League," I said.

Blink, blink, blink. "The what?"

"The League. You know what I mean."

"No," he said. "No, I don't."

"Sure you do, Johnny. No point in lying about it."

"I'm not lying. I…you mean the Kinsmen—?"

The last word came out in a snipped-off whisper, as if he hadn't meant to say it and he was trying to bite it back as it tumbled out. He scrubbed a dirty hand over his face, smearing and blackening his sweat. He wasn't looking at me anymore.

I said, "Tell me about the Kinsmen, Johnny."

"No. I don't know nothing about them…"

"Come on, we both know you do. Gene Ballard's a member—how about your boss? He one of them, too?"

Headshake.

"Who else in town belongs?"

Blink, blink. Headshake.

"Who's leader of the Kinsmen? What is it they—"

He came driving up out of his chair, so suddenly and with such violence that he kicked over the space heater and made me take a couple of quick steps backward to get clear. "Leave me alone! I don't know nothing, I don't want to talk about those... I don't want to talk to you anymore, just leave me alone!" He blundered past me and out into the rain and was gone around the far corner of the garage.

Kinsmen, I thought.

Another name for the Christian National Emancipation League? Or another racist group, affiliated with the League, maybe, that was even more militant? Whatever they were, the Kinsmen were bad news—

bad enough to scare hell out of a husky twenty-year-old kid.

* * *

There was a public telephone mounted on the front wall of the general store, and I used it to call the San Francisco *Chronicle.* Joe DeFalco wasn't in, even though it was four-twenty. The woman I spoke to didn't know where he'd gone but she thought he'd be back. I gave her my name and said to tell him I'd call again before six.

Downstreet, the lights from the Modoc Cafe put a saffron tint on the gathering twilight. In close to the big front window, the rain had a burnished silver cast. I took the car down there to keep from getting any wetter than I already was.

Lena was on duty now and Andrea was gone. A man and a woman sat in the last of the left-hand row of booths; they were the only customers. I claimed the first of the right-hand booths. Lena took her time coming over to me, and when she did she left her professional smile behind. But there was no hostility in her expression. Just a kind of guarded blankness, like an empty house with its security alarm switched on.

"Persistent, aren't you?" she said.

"I get paid to be."

"Maybe you don't know it, but this isn't a good place to be persistent in. Creekside, I mean."

"No? Why not?"

"People here don't like outsiders."

"I know. Especially outsiders who ask a lot of questions about things nobody wants to talk about."

"That's right."

"How about you? What do you think of persistent outsiders?"

"I think I don't want to answer any more questions."

"Not even to save a couple of lives?"

"If those kids are still alive."

"You think they might not be?"

"I hope they are."

"So do I. So do their families."

Small silence. Then she asked, "You find out anything?"

"A little. His name's Rob Compton and they're planning to be married."

"That's no surprise."

"But you don't approve?"

"Marriage is a shitty proposition when both people belong to the same race. Black and white makes it twice as shitty."

"They don't think so. It's their mistake to make anyway, if it is a mistake. Right?"

"I guess." Lena nibbled at her lower lip, the way you do when you're trying to make up your mind about something. "You going to order? Can't keep sitting here if you don't."

"Coffee. Black."

She went away, came back with the coffee. And with something else for me too: conscience and innate decency had won out over fear and self-interest, for a change.

"Last Friday night," she said, leaning close so her voice wouldn't carry, "just after those kids left, Mike Cermak came in. He passed right by them and the two guys they were talking to out front."

"Uh-huh. And how does this Mike Cermak feel about answering questions from outsiders?"

"He's an outsider himself. At least, he wasn't born in these mountains and he keeps to himself. Mike's okay."

"Where can I find him?"

"Up at the end of Cedar Street. Last house where it dead ends."

"Cedar Street is where?"

"Back toward the highway, south. Off Main."

"All right to use your name with him?"

"You'd better, if you want him to talk to you."

I might have asked her about the Kinsmen—the question was in my mind—but the front door opened just then and the wet wind blew in a trio of men, all roughly dressed and none familiar to me. Lena knew them and she didn't seem to want them to know she'd been talking to me; she waved and called out names, moved off in their direction without looking my way again.

Just as well, I thought as I finished my coffee. The way things stood now, Lena was at least marginally on my side, the only ally I'd found in this dark little town. If she knew anything about the Kinsmen, it wasn't likely she'd confide it to me; and if I put any pressure on her, she would curl up inside her protective shell and shut me out entirely. Conscience and innate decency only go so far in this cover-your-ass society of ours.

14.

Cedar Street was a twisty little roadway—
half paved, half gravel, all chuckholes—that
climbed onto the hillside above the village.
It started out fairly wide but by the time
I reached its terminus, after about half a
mile, it was so narrow two normal-sized
cars couldn't have passed each other without swapping paint scrapes.

There was only one house up there,
built on a couple of acres of cleared ground
behind a crazy-quilt fence that was part
grape-stake, part chicken wire, and part
rough-wood poles. The house was old, badly in need of paint, and seemed to list about
five degrees to the south; lights in its facing windows pressed palely against the early
darkness. The yard in front and around on
one side was an incredible clutter of things
spread out under tin-roofed lean-tos: car
parts, tools, stacks of cordwood, lengths

of pipe, plumbing fixtures, appliances, hundreds of other items less easily identifiable. A homemade sign on the gate said: *Cermak's Bargains—Buy, Sell, Trade—Free Pickup and Delivery.*

The man who opened the door to my knock was not quite a stranger: he was the aging hippie I'd tried to talk to at the general store on Wednesday. He didn't look any more cooperative tonight. Not hostile, just carefully neutral—like Switzerland. Another cover-your-ass citizen.

"Mike Cermak?"

Small nod.

"Remember me?" I said. "I'm the man who—"

"I know who you are. What do you want?"

"A few minutes of your time."

"I can't help you, man. I don't know anything about those college kids."

"Maybe you know more than you think. Lena down at the cafe said you'd talk to me. How about it?"

"Talk to you about what?"

"Last Friday night. Those kids were out front of the cafe, talking to a couple of guys, when you got there. You passed right by them."

"So?"

"So maybe you can tell me who the guys are and what the conversation was about."

Silence for a time, while he did a little struggling with himself. Then he said reluctantly, "All right, come inside. Too damn cold out here."

The interior of the house had the same junk-shop clutter as the front yard—a mix of private possessions and goods for sale. A wood-burning stove made the room too warm. A fattish woman with long braided hair sat on a scruffy sofa, making something that looked to be a beadwork purse. Cermak gestured to her and she got up without a word and left the room, taking her beadwork and a half full glass of wine with her.

Cermak said to me, "I can't tell you their names."

"The two men who were talking to the kids?"

"Yeah."

"Can't or won't tell me?"

"Can't. Don't know who they are."

"They don't live around here? Strangers to you?"

"…Not exactly strangers."

"So they do live in the area. Where?"

No answer.

"You don't know or you don't want to say?"

This time I got an evasion: "Won't do you any good to look them up."

"No? Why not?"

"They won't talk to you."

"Why not? Because they're Kinsmen?"

A muscle twitched in Cermak's cheek. He went to where another half-full glass of wine sat on an end table; drained the glass before he looked at me again. "What do you know about the Kinsmen?"

"Not as much as I'd like to. What do *you* know about them?"

"Nothing, man. They're none of my business."

"They're racists," I said. "That makes them everybody's business."

"Not mine. Different universes."

"I'll bet you didn't feel that way in the sixties. I'll bet you did a little civil rights marching back then."

"The sixties are dead, a long time dead. I'm older and wiser now."

"Older anyway."

"I don't need any bullshit lectures, man. You don't know me and I don't know you."

"But you do know the Kinsmen."

He avoided my eyes again, poured some more wine. But sooner or later he was going to tell me what I wanted to know, and we both knew it. Otherwise he wouldn't have let me in the house in the first place.

I said, "The two men last Friday night. Were they hassling the kids?"

"Some," he said. "Bad scene."

"Because she was white and he was black."

"Yeah."

"Taunts, threats—what?"

"Taunts. They called him a nigger and worse."

"What did he say?"

"He didn't say anything. She wanted to argue with them but the black kid took her arm and hustled her away."

"The other two follow them?"

"No. Yelled some more shit and then got in their jeep and split."

"In the opposite direction?"

"That's right. Out of town."

"You see the kids again that night?"

"No."

"The next day? Any time since?"

"No."

"How about the two in the jeep?"

"Not that night and not since," Cermak said. "They don't come into town much—none of them do. Those two soldiers were only in for an emergency buy at the hardware store."

"You don't mean real soldiers. Paramilitary types?"

"…Yeah."

"Describe them for me."

"Young and lily white, like most of them out there. Wearing soldier shit—camouflage fatigues, combat boots."

"Armed?"

"I didn't see any guns."

"You said, 'like most of them out there.' Out where?"

No response.

"Come on, Mike, where can I find them? Some kind of camp where they all live, is that it?"

Cermak worked on his wine for a time. Then, abruptly, he blew out his breath in an angry sigh and said, "Screw it. All right, yeah, they got a camp back in the woods. Big place, been building it for a year now."

"Where in the woods?"

"Timberline Road. Seven or eight miles west of town."

"Sounds like you've been there," I said.

"I was. Once. They bought a bunch of stuff from me before I knew who they were and I delivered it. Once was enough."

"What kind of place is it?"

"Looks like one of those church retreats, at least from a distance. Cabins, big meeting hall, storage sheds, church building with a cross on top."

"But it's more than that, right?"

"Lot more. Big bad bummer."

"Paramilitary training ground?"

"Right on."

"Weapons?"

"Only ones I saw were on the guards patrolling the gate and grounds. Machine pistols and assault rifles."

"How many people living there?"

"Couple of dozen back then. Probably more now."

"All men?"

"No. A few women, even a couple of kids."

"Who'd you deal with? Who seemed to be in charge?"

"Somebody called 'The Colonel.' Don't know his name."

"Describe him."

"Tall, thin, white-haired, about fifty. Looked and acted like a fucking Nazi."

"Okay. The name Richard Artemus Chaffee mean anything to you?"

"No."

"He's head of an outfit called the Christian National Emancipation League."

"Racist flyer in the general store," Cermak said. "Yeah."

"But you're not aware of any connection between the League and the Kinsmen?"

"No."

"Kinsmen own the land the camp is on? Lease it?"

"Can't tell you that. It used to belong to a big cattle rancher, maybe still does."

"What's his name?"

"McMahon. George McMahon."

"Know anything about him, whether or not he's one of them?"

"No. He keeps to himself. Most do around here."

"But the Kinsmen have been recruiting locals, haven't they? Holding open meetings, preaching racism?"

"Some. They're cool about it."

"With much success?"

"More than you'd think. You can sell any kind of shit to some of the stupid bastards in these hills."

"Gene Ballard, for instance?"

"That creep."

"Who else in Creekside?"

Cermak shook his head. "Gave you enough names. Christ, man, my old lady and me got to live here. Maybe you'd just better split, huh? Do what you have to someplace else."

He'd been nervous all along; the sudden closing up was not surprising. I'd been lucky to get him to talk as much as he had. I said, "All right. Just tell me how to get to Timberline Road and the McMahon ranch and I'll leave you alone."

He told me and I copied the directions down in my notebook. At the door he said with a kind of self-mockery, "Peace, brother," and shut it in my face. Flower child grown old and gone to seed. Dropped out a long time ago and wanted to stay that way: drink wine and smoke dope with his old lady, sell his bargains, and let the rest of the world slide by. But there was still a little love and caring left in him, still a little of the old sixties philosophy. Hell, by Creekside standards he and Lena were right up there with Mother Teresa in the humanitarian department.

15.

From the public phone outside the Creek-side General Store, I put in another long-distance call to the S.F. *Chronicle.* And this time Joe DeFalco was at his desk.

"I got the poop you wanted," he said. "Actually, shit is a much more appropriate word."

"Yeah. Talk to me, Joe."

"Christian National Emancipation League," he said. "Operating under that name for about three years, but founded a good ten years ago by this guy Chaffee. He used to be a salesman down in the Central Valley. Gave up his job and became a preacher in 'eighty-two, courtesy of one of those outfits that ordain by mail. Opened up a temple outside Turlock called Church of the Emancipator, preached a combination of fundamentalist religion and racist dogma. Usual white-race-is-the-chosen-race crap. Not many followers, not until he began to de-emphasize religion and come down heavy on the white supremacist angle. Then the Church of the Emancipator turned into the Christian National Emancipation League."

"Many members?" I asked.

"No way of getting an exact count. Probably not more than a hundred."

"What's their philosophy? Separatism through violence?"

"Not openly, no. Just separatism."

"So they're not a militant outfit?"

"I repeat, not openly. These hate groups are all militant to one degree or another. Posse Comitatus, neo-Nazi Skinheads, the Klan, the NAAWP, the White Aryan Resistance…all of them."

"No direct surface links to violent acts or weapons offenses?"

"No. The League doesn't seem to be one of the real whacko groups like the Aryan Brotherhood—you know, the bunch that murdered the Denver radio show host a few years ago—or Butler's 'Heavenly Reich' in Idaho. But under the surface…who knows?"

"They refer to themselves by any name other than the Christian National Emancipation League?"

"Such as?"

"The Kinsmen."

"Nothing about that in the public record," DeFalco said, "but it could be. The title of the bulletin Chaffee puts out is *The Kinsmen Monthly.* Why?"

"There's a covert racist bunch up here calling themselves the Kinsmen. It may or may not be the same crowd."

"Affiliate or offshoot of the League, maybe. These bastards are always splitting off and forming new cells, like goddamn amoeba germs."

"You find any connection between the League and Creekside? Or word of League activity in Modoc or Lassen counties?"

"No to both. Just what kind of outfit is the Kinsmen?"

"I'm not sure yet," I said, "but they've built a camp back deep in the wilderness and it seems at least partially to be a para-military operation." I repeated what Mike Cermak had told me about the place.

"Jesus," DeFalco said. "How long has this camp been there?"

"About a year."

"Population growing? Recruiting locals on the QT?"

"Looks that way."

"That's how Butler got started in Hayden Lake. And the Aryan Brotherhood at Whidbey Island up in Washington state. Indoctrination centers and paramilitary and terrorist training grounds. You have any idea of who's in charge up there?"

"Somebody called 'The Colonel.' No name yet. Tall, thin, white-haired, fiftyish. Probably ex-military."

"Uh-huh. A lot of these radical anar-chists are."

I said, "They got the land they're using from a local rancher—McMahon, George McMahon. That name ring any bells?"

"…No. You think he's one of them?"

"Good possibility."

"I'll do some more digging, see what I can find out about him and The Colonel."

"Thanks, Joe."

"*De nada*. You've got me plenty interested, pal. What's your next move?"

"Go out to McMahon's ranch tomorrow, see if he'll talk to me. And scout the area where the Kinsmen have their nest."

"If it is a Hayden Lake or Whidbey Island kind of nest," he said, "they're crazies that don't mind killing people. May already have started killing people…those missing college kids of yours. Watch your ass."

"I'll watch it," I said. "You be home tomorrow?"

"All weekend. And don't call just to pump me for information. If this thing is as big and nasty as it sounds, I want a piece of it—a public piece, exclusive. Deal?"

"Deal."

* * *

I drove back to the Northern Comfort Cabins; there was nothing else for me to do tonight but hole up. At first I tried to read, then I tried to watch the flickery picture on the ancient TV, then I lay there and listened to the rain. Then I called Kerry's number, but she wasn't home: working late on her "Shirt Happens" account. Restlessness prodded me out of there, into an aimless walk in the cold drizzle. And after fifteen minutes, the cold drizzle prodded me back into the damn cabin.

The Kinsmen...Creekside...the disappearance of Allison Shay and Rob Compton. The three were interconnected, all right; had to be. Those two soldier types last Friday night—too disciplined to go after the kids right away, but they could have returned to the village the next morning and followed Allison and Rob when they left and then waylaid them somewhere. Or they might have just reported the presence of a white woman and a black man to The Colonel, and he'd dispatched other soldiers to do the waylaying. That kind of mindless, knee-jerk racial violence was all too possible if the Kinsmen were as militant as they seemed to be.

And yet, I couldn't fit Allison's MG into the scenario. Why run the risk of driving the car all the way to Eureka? Too far a distance and too unnecessary a ploy; out of character for a paramilitary outfit. They weren't trying to hide their presence in the area, not if they were openly recruiting locals; and with nothing to tie them or their camp directly to the kids' disappearance, there was no need for a fancy smokescreen. If they'd killed Allison and Rob, why not just bury the car along with the bodies, someplace deep in the wilderness nearby? There was more to this business than execution murder by a band of white supremacists. I felt it, and I knew I was right, but I couldn't seem to figure an explanation, given the facts I had gathered so far, that made any better sense.

16.

Timberline Road was backcountry, all right. Deep backcountry. "Seven or eight miles west of Creekside," Mike Cermak had said. Maybe so, but the route you had to travel to get there was so circuitous the distance seemed twice as long. Cermak's directions weren't too good either; I made a pair of wrong turns, got so badly lost once I had to stop at a farmhouse for help in putting myself back on the right track. Nor did the weather help matters any. More rain this morning, coupled with a thick undulant mist that obscured the hilly terrain and filled every hollow as if with mounds of half-frozen smoke. Altogether I spent an hour on a network of rough, narrow lanes before I finally found a signpost that said Timberline Road...and alongside it, another that proclaimed *Not a Through Road.*

There were no houses along there, or at least none I could see and no driveways or branch lanes to get to one. Just thick stands of pine and fir, broken now and then by rocky meadows and hillsides patched with second-growth timber and notched with deadfalls. Old logging area, old logging road. Empty wilderness now, remote—just the right kind of terrain for a paramilitary outpost.

I followed Timberline Road for nearly a mile, through dips and curves and several switchbacks. Down and up and back down again. The road surface kept worsening, until it was so heavily pocked that I had to slow to a crawl. I rolled around another tight turn—and fifty yards ahead the road came to an abrupt end. Or rather, free access came to an abrupt end: a semaphore lift gate, like the ones you see at railroad crossings, had been erected across it. Mounted on the lift bar was a big STOP sign, and next to it, another sign that had been semiprofessionally painted in crimson letters. That one said:

PRIVATE PROPERTY
NO ENTRANCE
WITHOUT PERMISSION
WHITES ONLY ALLOWED!

I stopped the car, sat there for a minute or so with the engine running and the wipers clacking away. Beyond the lift gate, trees had been cleared to open up a hundred-yard-wide section of meadowland; a long, high chainlink fence ran through the middle of the cleared area, with another gate in it double-barring the road. The fence and the second gate were topped with strands of wicked-looking barbed wire. The effect was of a military no-man's land, of the type that used to exist along the border between West and East Germany.

There was nobody manning either gate, nobody in sight on either side of the chainlink fence. Past the fence, the road was visible for another seventy-five yards before it vanished into a thick stand of Douglas fir. The buildings that formed the camp were well hidden behind the trees and the drear gray wall of rain and mist.

Well, I thought, let's see what a little snooping buys.

In a clip under the dash was the .38 Smith & Wesson Bodyguard I had bought recently as an emergency weapon. I don't like guns much but sometimes they're necessary; I'd been in situations before where I had need of one and I'd finally wised up to the fact that continuing to go about my business unprepared was a damned fool thing to do. One of those situations now? No. I was one man and there were Christ knew how many whackos with Christ knew how many guns somewhere close by. Carrying heat on their turf was begging for an early grave.

I shut the car down, got out. The wind, dead-cold out here, blew rain into my face; I could hear it making empty muttering sounds in the trees. Nothing else to hear. And still nothing to see as I crossed to the lift bar, climbed over it, and approached the fence.

The gate there had a double padlock on it. I looked at the strands of barbed wire. I might be able to get up and over without cutting myself up too badly, even at my age, but it wasn't worth the effort. I would really be guilty of trespassing then. Cermak hadn't mentioned anything about killer dogs on the loose in the compound, but for all I knew—

"What you want here, mister?"

He didn't yell the words; he didn't have to because he was not that far behind me. I turned, slowly, with the hackles going up on my neck. He must have come from the trees off on the left, but he'd done it with all the stealth of a commando. He looked like a commando, too: camouflage jacket and trousers, heavy black Army boots, a soldier's cap worn backwards as if in some kind of protest against standard military procedure. He was young, not much more than voting age, and fair-skinned and ice-eyed. The weapon he held across his body was a semiautomatic assault rifle with a clip that looked a foot long. It wasn't pointed at me because it didn't need to be. He could spray enough bullets with that thing to cut down twenty men in a matter of seconds.

He walked toward me, stiff-backed and wary. I lifted my hands, palms outward, to shoulder level. He wasn't alone on sentry duty out here: I could feel eyes on my back, eyes and more weapons. The sensation made my body hunch involuntarily inside my clothing.

When the kid got close enough for a good look at me, I saw his face pinch up and an ugliness come into his eyes. I'm an olive-skinned Italian—and he'd been conditioned to hate anybody with skin darker than his own. I told myself I wasn't dark enough to trigger him, that he'd be too disciplined for that, but it was not much comfort. How the hell can you predict what a gun-bearing racist will do?

"What do you want here?" he said again. Hard, clipped, but with an edge of nervousness I didn't like.

"Nothing. I don't want anything." I made myself sound scared, the bewildered kind of scared, and apologetic. "I was just out driving around…you know, exploring the countryside, and I—"

"This is private property," the kid said. "Can't you read?"

"Sure, I saw the sign. I thought it meant no admittance on the other side of the fence."

"Why'd you get out of your car? Why'd you come walking up here?"

"I don't know," I said, "I was just curious. I mean, you come on this place all of a sudden and it makes you curious. I thought I'd walk up and take a peek through the gate, that's all. Just a quick peek." I widened the spread of my hands. "I didn't mean any harm."

He thought it over. But he didn't have any reason to disbelieve me; I was a man pushing sixty, alone, non-threatening. He said, "Private property, like the sign says. All of this here."

"Sure. Sure thing. What's going on, anyway?"

"Nothing's going on."

"Well, I mean, you're carrying that rifle and the sign says Whites Only Allowed..."

"You live around here, mister?"

"Not yet, no. I'm thinking about moving up to this part of the world though. Too many blacks down in the Bay Area where I live now."

"Too many niggers everywhere," he said.

"Whites Only Allowed...that's the kind of place I like," I lied. "What have you got here? Some kind of retreat or what?"

He didn't say anything. Just watched me with flat blue eyes that didn't blink despite the rain blowing into them.

"Private?" I asked. "Or can anybody join up?"

"Anybody can if they qualify. I don't think you qualify."

"No? Why not?"

"You're a dago, that's why. Dago's not white."

I could feel the heat rise in me. "I've got Italian blood," I said carefully, "but I'm still white."

"Not as far as we're concerned," the kid said. "Go on, get out of here. We don't want your kind around here."

"Just like that, huh?"

"Just like that." He moved his weapon a little. "You're trespassing. Get off our property and don't come back if you know what's good for you."

I had an irrational impulse to rush him, gun or no gun—hurt him with my hands. It didn't last long; I'm not suicidal. I said, "I'm gone, kid, long gone. I don't make the same mistake twice."

"Better not," he said, but he was talking to my back.

When I got to the car he still stood up there in no-man's land, watching me, the assault rifle at port arms. Evil in the rain. With more evil hidden away behind him, eating at the wilderness like a cancer.

17.

The McMahon ranch was easier to find than the Kinsmen camp, but when I got there I learned even less than I had on Timberline Road. It had been built on mostly open land in the same general area, a few miles to the south—a sprawling place, at least a dozen buildings of varying sizes tucked away behind chainlink fencing. All of the buildings were painted a gleaming white. There might not have been any racial connotation to the paint job, but I wouldn't have wanted to bet on it.

A gate barred entrance here, too: the electronic variety. On one of the support pillars was an intercom thing; I used it to call the main house. A male voice answered. When I gave my name and asked to see George McMahon on an important matter, the voice said Mr. McMahon was busy and not seeing anyone without an appointment. I said the important matter had to do with the Kinsmen, but that didn't buy me anything. The voice informed me in chillier tones that Mr. McMahon was not seeing anyone for any reason, and cut me off before I could make another pitch.

So. Back in the car, back to Creekside, out to Highway 395. It was past noon when I reached Susanville. I stopped for gas, and from a phone booth at the station I called Joe DeFalco at his home in Daly City.

"Sounds like another Hayden Lake, all right," he said when I finished telling him about my encounter with the Aryan soldier. He sounded pretty excited. Why not; it was armchair intrigue for him.

"Yeah. I can almost hear you licking your chops."

"Big stories don't shake out very often," he said. "I've always wanted a Pulitzer."

"You and every other newspaper hack."

"Listen, I think I've got an ID on the guy running the camp up there—The Colonel. If I'm right, he's a hell of a big fish."

"How so?"

"Wanted by the FBI for masterminding the theft of a truckload of weapons from a federal armory in Arkansas a couple of years ago. There's also an Oklahoma state fugitive warrant on him—suspicion of conspiracy to commit murder."

"White supremacist ties?"

"Oh hell yes. His name is Darnell, Colonel Benjamin Darnell. Ex-Vietnam vet, ex-mercenary soldier in Latin America and Africa. Thrown out of the U.S. Army for conduct unbecoming an officer...racially motivated attack on a black sergeant. Reputed to have spent some time at Butler's Aryan Nations hideaway as a training officer. And here's the clincher: His brother-in-law is cut from the same miserable cloth and has been linked to a couple of California-based racist groups, one of them being the Christian National Emancipation League."

"Bad," I said. I was thinking of Marian Shay.

"And liable to get worse if something isn't done."

"What about George McMahon? Ties there, too?"

"Not that I can find so far, but I'd be surprised if he wasn't one of them. Hard-core right-winger, worth a couple of million bucks. Used to be active in ultracon-servative politics in that part of the state."

"Used to be?"

"Dropped out about five years ago. Turned into something of a recluse since then—very low profile."

"Recluse, hell. Racist all along, went the hardline route five years ago and got hooked up with Chaffee and Darnell."

"I read it that way too," DeFalco agreed. "I'll keep trying to confirm."

"Do that. Anything else?"

"Not much. I called the editor of the North Corner *Gazette* this morning—that's a bi-weekly in Susanville—and asked him some pointed questions. He admitted to hearing whispers about a racist group infil-trating the area. But he said he couldn't pin them down."

"He must not have tried very hard."

"He didn't. He's an old-timer—ambition all dried up, disinclined to open up a cesspool in his own backyard."

"The ostrich syndrome."

"Lot of that going around these days. But he did tell me one thing that ties in. There've been several isolated racial incidents in the Corner in recent months."

"What kind of incidents?"

"Vandalism at a Vietnamese restaurant in Alturas, cross burning at the home of a black family near the Oregon border, hate mail sent to half a dozen Asian families. No overt violence—not yet. You can smell it coming though."

"The Kinsmen," I said.

"Sure. But there's no proof it's an organized hate campaign. The authorities have it pegged as random teenage activity."

"No proof of anything yet," I said, "except that maybe Colonel Darnell is hiding out at the Kinsmen camp. And maybe he isn't; for all we know, he did his job here and went somewhere else. The man I talked to saw him months ago, not recently."

"Can you find out one way or the other?"

"I can try."

"Be better if we knew that, or had proof of conspiracy or *some* kind of felony, before we call in the FBI. Easier for the Feds to take the Kinsmen down, better story for me, more glory for you."

"I don't want any glory," I said. "All I want is to find those missing kids. Alive."

"I know. But the way this thing is shaping up...well, I don't have to tell you it doesn't look good."

"Nothing looks good up here right now," I said grimly. "Not a frigging thing."

After we rang off I considered calling Marian Shay. But I couldn't bring myself to do it. I was in no frame of mind to listen to the fear in her voice, to perpetuate what seemed more and more to be false hopes. So I looked up Mike Cermak's number and called him instead.

At first I thought he was going to hang up on me, but he didn't. There was a silence and when he spoke again he sounded wearily resigned—the voice of a man who has done something against his better judgment and is morally certain that he is going to regret it for the rest of his life.

"The man called The Colonel," I said. "When did you last see him?"

"Day I was out at the camp. I told you."

"How long ago was that?"

"Last summer. Late June, early July."

"Not even a glimpse of him since in the village?"

"No. I've never seen him in Creekside. None of them come in much. I told you that, too."

"Do you know if he's still at the camp?"

"No. How would I know?"

"Any other local tradesman make a delivery out there besides you? Recently, I mean. Within the past couple of weeks."

"I doubt it. Don't ask me about other people in Creekside, man. Ask them. I don't pay attention to anybody's business but my own."

I thought about going back to Creekside right away, asking Lena and some of the other citizens about The Colonel, but there didn't seem to be much point in it. Given the fact that there were federal and state warrants out on Darnell, it was probable he never spent time in any town. And if a Creeksider had seen him at the camp recently, that person was probably a racist and wouldn't tell me a damn thing. The only way I could find out for sure if Darnell was still around was to infiltrate the camp and see for myself—and that, sure as hell, would be a suicide mission.

Frustrated, I hunted up the offices of the North Corner *Gazette*. And of course they were closed for the weekend. Lettering on the door gave the editor's name as Walter Harmon. I looked him up in the local directory; he and his address were both listed. But when I found his house he wasn't there—or at least his wife said he wasn't there. Gone fishing, she said. In the rain? More likely he was somewhere inside with his head in a bucket of sand.

I wasted the rest of the afternoon in the local library, poking through back issues of the *Gazette* and the other small newspapers in the area. The racial incidents were mentioned—five of them over a period of three months. As DeFalco had said, none involved overt violence against an individual; but that meant nothing. It only takes one set of volatile circumstances to trigger racial violence, and a black man and a white woman in a village like Creekside was about as volatile as you could get. The most recent issue of the *Gazette,* published two days ago, carried a brief mention of the disappearance. There was nothing else of interest in any of the issues I scanned through.

Five o'clock. And in spite of my mood I was hungry; I hadn't eaten anything all day. I found a steak restaurant on the outskirts of town and took my time with a meal, but it was still only six-forty when I came out. I had no desire to return to Creekside yet, so I hied myself to the local theater and took in a movie. A lousy movie, one of those mindless action flicks filled with spectacular vehicle crashes and people and things getting blown up every few minutes. Lots of torn flesh, lots of blood. The rest of the audience seemed to love it; I walked out before it was over.

Entertainment? Hell no. There's nothing entertaining about blood and pain and abused flesh. Not at the best of times and sure as hell not when your job is dealing with the real thing in the real world.

18.

And I had to deal with the real thing again a lot sooner than I expected. It was waiting for me when I got back to the Northern Comfort Cabins.

I was still the only paying guest; the courtyard was deserted except for the Bartholomews' Buick parked behind the office building, and there were no lights showing in any of the cabins. The office was a little island of pale, cheerless yellow blurred by rain that had slackened here to a fine wind-blown mist. The rear of the motel grounds, where Cabin Eleven waited, was ink-black outside the burrowing cones of my head-lamps. When I stopped the car and shut the lights off, it was so dark I could barely make out the shape of the cabin a few feet away.

I pulled my coat collar up, got out, locked the car, and exchanged the car keys for the door key as I turned toward the cabin. The brittle mountain wind made skirling, rattling noises in the evergreens nearby, but I heard the men coming anyway. If they'd been professionals, I wouldn't have heard them. But they were amateurs, and in their haste they made noise—enough noise so that I had time to swing around toward them and brace my body against the cabin wall before they attacked me.

Black shapes, two of them, bulky, one with something upraised in his hand… grunts, a thin giggling laugh, a voice spitting the words "Teach you to come where you ain't wanted!"…the smell of sweat and dry wool: jumbled impressions in the two or three seconds before it started. Then the one with the weapon swung at my head and the rest of it seemed to happen at warp speed.

I ducked under the swing, kicked that one in the leg; he yelled and stumbled back away from me. The other man hit me a glancing blow over the heart that didn't hurt much, didn't do any damage. I jabbed at him, missed, jabbed again and felt my knuckles hit bone and the shock of impact like an eruption in my armpit. But it didn't hurt him much either; he grunted, swore, tried to drive his knee into my crotch. He didn't have enough leverage, but I did: when his knee came up I turned my body and side-kicked his other shin. That staggered him. I managed to hit him somewhere in the face with my fist, a solid, meaty blow that knocked him down, mewling.

The first one was back by then, with a vengeance. Whatever he was swinging caught me on the left shoulder and the arm instantly went numb. He tried to club me again; this time I was able to avoid the swing, heard whatever the thing was smash against the wall behind my head. His arm was up where I could see it and I got a grip on the woolen sleeve of his coat and yanked the arm down, hard, at the same time bringing a leg up to meet it. I heard and felt his wrist break. Heard him scream, heard the club clatter on the wet ground.

I shoved him away, pawed rain out of my face so I could look for the second one.

But he'd had enough of me. I saw him for a few seconds, getting to his feet, swaying like a sapling in the wind, then he merged with the blackness and I was listening to the pound of his shoes on the gravel, running away.

The one with the broken wrist yelled in a high-pitched voice, "You son of a bitch, I'll get you for this!" I yelled back at him, "Come on then, come on come on," but he was all through, too. He lurched away, fell down, scrambled up, and was gone. I would have given chase if it weren't for the numbness in my left arm and shoulder. As it was I leaned back against the cabin wall with my face upturned, sucking at the moist air. My chest felt tight, hot. The hissing blood-pound in my ears was like surf in a storm.

Lucky. That was my first thought when I could think clearly again. Lucky I wasn't lying on the ground right now with a broken head. Lucky those two amateurs were busts when it came to nighttime slugging.

Distantly a car engine roared to life and tires bit squealing into pavement. So long, you bastards, I thought. Thinking about coming back later with reinforcements? You'll wish you hadn't if you do.

Some feeling began to return to my left arm, a hot tingling that made my fingertips throb. Pretty soon I could move it all right, hands and fingers, too; nothing broken. I shoved off the wall, leaned gingerly on the car while I unlocked the driver's door. From under the dash I unclipped the .38 revolver. And the flashlight I keep there with it; I had lost the cabin key sometime during the skirmish and it wasn't likely I could find it unaided in the dark.

Even with the torch, it took me almost five minutes to locate the key: it was half-hidden in a puddle. I also spotted the thing the one slugger had tried to brain me with—a three-foot length of stove-wood. The rain had quickened again and the wind had gone gusty; the storm was all there was to hear now. Plenty of noise in the past few minutes, though, and plenty of shifting arrows of light from my flash—and yet no sign of either of the Bartholomews. If they'd heard or seen the fight, they didn't want any part of it or its aftermath. Mrs. Bartholomew: *The Lord's business, not mine.* Yeah.

Shivering, I keyed open the cabin door. Warm enough inside but I turned the space heater up anyway, as high as it would go. I locked the door and wedged the only chair under the knob and then went into the bathroom cubicle for a damage check.

Not too bad. Scrape on my neck, a big gathering bruise on my shoulder, a swelling on one knuckle. I stripped and stood under a hot shower for a while to ease some of the shoulder soreness. When I came out I put on my robe and moved the chair over under the window and sat there looking out past the edge of the shade, the .38 on the table next to me.

I sat there for a long time. They didn't come back. Nobody drove into the lot, nobody came out of the office building— nothing at all happened. I did a lot of thinking, sitting there. The reason for the attack was clear enough: I was getting too close to the truth about what had happened to Allison Shay and Rob Compton. That giggling laugh from the slugger whose wrist I'd snapped—Gene Ballard, no mistake. Both Johnny and Mike Cermak had pretty much confirmed that Ballard was a Kinsmen recruit…and yet I couldn't see it as a Kinsmen-ordered assault. Trying to beat up somebody in an effort to scare him off is a neophyte's ploy, not a paramilitary one. If the Kinsmen had already murdered two people, they wouldn't hesitate to murder a third to protect themselves; and they'd have sent trained soldiers to do it with guns, not amateurs armed with a piece of stove-wood.

So had Ballard been acting on his own? Or as a favor to somebody other than the Kinsmen? The second slugger, for instance—Art Maxe?

The more I thought, the more it seemed I had enough facts to work out the right answers; but my head hurt and I couldn't seem to separate the significant few from the insignificant majority. At midnight, fatigue drove me out of the chair and into bed. I was asleep in thirty seconds.

I slept hard and deep for four hours, and then woke up suddenly in a cold sweat. And with everything clear and sharp in my mind: What had happened to Allison and Rob. Who had made it happen and why. Even when and where.

Not just the facts but the whole truth had been in my head for days now. *Under* and *over* my head, too. Monsters hiding in plain sight that I just hadn't recognized for what they were.

Jesus. Sweet Jesus.

19.

Sunday morning.

Church bells began pealing, faint above the babble of the wind, a little before nine o'clock. I had been up for more than an hour by then, sitting stiff and sore at the front window, waiting. From this vantage point I had a full angled view of the back end of the office building.

The bells had been making their musical summons for about three minutes when the Bartholomews came out through the rear door. Him in a dark blue suit, his tie drawn so tightly that his wattles hung down in folds alongside the knot; her in a black and white dress and a boxy hat with some kind of feather poking out of it. On their way to church, all right. Both of them together because with me as the only guest, they didn't have any reason not to close the office for an hour or so this morning.

One hand tight on her arm, Bartholomew helped his wife into their old Buick. She was a little unsteady on her feet—the muddy ground over there, maybe, but more likely it was a few belts of pre-sermon gin. I watched him get in, start the car, let it warm up for a minute or so, then maneuver it around the building and out onto Main Street. He was a good driver, not too fast, not too slow, with a sure touch on the wheel.

I waited five minutes, in case they'd forgotten something. Then I went out into the chill, damp morning. The rain had quit sometime during the night but the smell and the feel of it were still in the air. Thick clouds swarmed overhead. I picked my way across the courtyard, dodging puddles like miniature lakes. The street out front was deserted now.

Bartholomew had locked the rear door, but it was not much of a lock; even with my sore shoulder and swollen finger I had it picked inside of thirty seconds. I went in fast, shut the door behind me. Kitchen.

Breakfast aromas clogged the air—toast, sausage, fried eggs. Strong in there too was the juniper-berry smell. Next to the sink, an empty carton of orange juice and an empty bottle of Beefeaters bore silent witness.

Three other rooms—living room, bedroom, bathroom—completed the Bartholomews' living space. All of the rooms were cramped and in need of tidying and cleaning. The bedroom drew me first, for no particular reason except a feeling that it was the right choice. And it was.

On the nightstand between twin beds was a well-used Gideon bible; and on the wall above an oak dresser hung a picture of Christ not unlike the one over the bed in Cabin Eleven. Symbols of faith, symbols of love. Directly underneath the picture, in two of the dresser drawers, I found the symbols of hate.

Computer-generated leaflets and pamphlets: desktop publishing of the worst kind. Newspapers: *The California Klan News,* the Posse Comitatus's *Posse Noose Report,* the White Aryan Resistance's *Aryan*

Vigil, the Christian National Emancipation League's *Kinsmen Monthly.* Cheaply printed paperback books, two of them with swastikas and death heads on the covers: *Warrant for Genocide, The Turner Diaries, Hitler Was Right!, White Power, Dead Coons.* Articles and printed slogans: "White People Built This Country—White People Are This Country." "Niggers and Kikes Beware!" "Make a List of Your Enemies." "Arm Yourselves Before It's Too Late." "The Only Way to Be Free of What Threatens You Is to Kill It—Learn to Kill Now!"

Jesus above and death below. It made me feel cold, dirty, and sad and angry and a little awed. How do they reconcile it? I thought. Pictures of the Savior, bible on the nightstand, and shit like this tucked away in a drawer. Read a little from the Book of Genesis or the Book of Job and then read a little from *White Power, Dead Coons.* How in God's name do they reconcile the two?

Maybe they don't, I thought then, maybe they can't and so they no longer even try. And maybe that's the key. To why she drinks, why he has the look of a reanimated corpse, why they live like this, why they did the things they did. Caught between two polar opposites, push-pull, for months and years until they were incapable of making any rational distinction; until they were self-indoctrinated to the point of paranoid schizophrenia. Now all they could do was respond to one set of stimuli or the other— love or hate, life or death, Christianity or anti-Christianity, but never one in relation to the other.

I was sweating now and my stomach had begun to kick. I wanted out of this place, to return to the cold clean air outside. But I wasn't done here yet. Not just yet.

The bedroom had nothing more for me. Neither did the living room. In a closet off the kitchen I found a pump shotgun, a Winchester .30-30, and an old Savage with iron sights. All three were loaded, and in there with them were at least a hundred extra rounds of ammunition for each—as if the Bartholomews were expecting a siege. "Arm Yourselves Before It's Too Late." "The

Only Way to Be Free of What Threatens You Is to Kill It—Learn to Kill Now!" That was exactly what they were expecting.

I looked for a handgun. No handgun. But there had to be at least one somewhere on the premises. The right one. They wouldn't have gotten rid of it, not people like them, not under any circumstances. Waste not, want not.

I found it out front, in a drawer under the office counter: a .32 Iver Johnson revolver, clean and oiled and fully loaded. The evidence said that the murder gun had to be a .32 or a small-bore .38. Okay.

Without touching the revolver, I shut the drawer and continued my search. The pocket of a fleece-lined jacket hanging from a hook on the kitchen wall yielded another piece of hard evidence—two pieces, actually. Greyhound bus ticket stubs, both stamped with last Sunday's date, one from Eureka to Redding and the other from Redding to Susanville.

When I finished looking at the stubs I returned them to the jacket pocket. If Bartholomew hadn't gotten rid of them over the past week, he wouldn't think to do it when he got home from church; it was likely he'd forgotten he still had them. They would be much more damning if the authorities found them just as I had.

Done. I opened the back door, didn't see anybody on the courtyard, reset the lock, and stepped outside. But I was wrong about the area being deserted—wrong twice, going in and now coming out. I hadn't taken more than a few paces when a hard voice said, "Hold it right there," and froze me in mid stride.

Art Maxe. Standing ten feet away, at the corner of the building, with a deer rifle pointed straight at my head.

20.

Second time in two days I'd been under a gun. This time I didn't put my hands up; I couldn't have gotten the left one up very high anyhow, as stiff as my shoulder was. I just stood there looking at him, waiting. If he wanted to shoot me there wasn't a damned thing I could do about it.

He said, "What the hell you think you're doing?"

"What do you think I'm doing?"

"I seen you bust in from down the road. Good thing I had my rifle in the truck. What'd you take in there?"

"Nothing."

"The hell. You took something, got it on you. Sheriff's deputies'll find it, by God."

So he wasn't going to shoot me. Some of the tension began to loosen in my chest and back. "Go ahead and call them," I said. "I was just about to do it myself."

"Sure you were."

"Plain truth. I found what I was looking for."

"Yeah? What's that?"

"More evidence."

"Evidence? Evidence of what?"

"That the Bartholomews murdered Allison Shay and Rob Compton last Friday night." The muzzle of Maxe's rifle dipped a little; he stared at me as if I'd suddenly changed shape, become an alien being. "Jesus Christ," he said. "You're crazy as a barn owl."

"Am I? I don't think so."

"Ed Bartholomew? Ruth? I known them thirty years...they wouldn't kill nobody."

"One of them did. Or maybe both of them."

"Why? For Chrissake, *why?*"

"Because they're hardline racists. Because Rob Compton was black and Allison Shay was white."

Maxe shook his head, more in confusion than negation. "Racists?"

"Members of a bunch of hate groups, including the Kinsmen. Like you, huh, Maxe?"

"Me? You think *I'm* a Kinsmen?"

"Aren't you?"

"No. Hell no. Sure, I went to one of their meetings with Gene Ballard, see what they were all about. But I didn't like what I heard. Still don't. I never went back."

"Then why did you and Ballard jump me last night?"

"Jump you? I don't know what you're talking about."

"No? Two men attacked me around nine-thirty, over in front of Cabin Eleven. They were waiting in one of the other cabins—had to be because it was raining and their clothing smelled dry and felt dry. The Bartholomews set it up. How else would the attackers get a key to an empty cabin? One of the men was Ballard; I recognized that laugh of his. I thought the other one was you."

"Thought wrong," Maxe said. "I was home last night. Ask my wife, if you don't believe me."

"All right, you weren't involved. But there's still the cover-up with Allison's car. You were part of that, no mistake."

"Bullshit. I don't know nothing about no cover-up."

"You lied about Allison and Rob picking up her MG on Saturday morning. They didn't pick it up; they couldn't have because they were already dead by then."

Headshake. Maxe was no mental giant; confusion was plain on his craggy face, as if he couldn't quite come to terms with all I was telling him.

"You did lie," I said, "we both know that. Why, if you had nothing to do with the murder or the cover-up?"

"Ed…he come down to the station that morning. Asked if their car was ready, said if it was he'd take it back to the motel. Said them two kids was still in bed and he wanted to get rid of 'em and if he brought their car right up to the door, maybe that would do it."

"Why did he say he wanted to get rid of them?"

"Him and Ruth didn't like the idea of a white woman and a...nigger sleeping together in one of their cabins. Said he wouldn't have put 'em up if he'd known the boy was a nigger. Said he didn't find it out until just that morning or he'd have got rid of 'em sooner..." Maxe wet his lips. "Jesus," he said.

"So you let him have the MG. What did he say then?"

"Then?"

"To get you to lie about who picked it up."

"Said he didn't want anybody to know he was fetching their car for them, didn't want anybody saying Ed Bartholomew fetched for a nigger and his white whore. Put it to me as a favor. I didn't see no harm in it—why should I? So I said all right, if anybody asked I'd say they come and got the car themselves."

The rifle muzzle was all the way down now, pointed at the ground between us. The last of my tension was gone, too. Maxe was telling the truth down the line; I was sure of it.

He said, "What'd Ed do with it—the MG?"

"Drove it to Eureka and abandoned it, to make it look like the kids disappeared over there. Sometime that day, Saturday. On Sunday he took a bus from Eureka to Redding and another from Redding to Susanville; I found the ticket stubs. His wife probably picked him up in Susanville. She does drive, doesn't she?"

"Yeah," Maxe said. "Not too far, the way she drinks, but Susanville…yeah." He ran his free hand through the tangle of his hair. Shook his head again. "I still ain't sure I believe it."

"You'd better believe it. It's what happened."

"Where? Where'd it happen?"

"The shooting? Cabin Eleven, the one the kids stayed in. The one I've been staying in."

"How you know that? How you know they was shot?"

"Come over there with me and I'll show you."

I took a couple of slow steps. The rifle muzzle stayed down. When I kept going Maxe moved too, jerkily, and fell into step beside me.

Inside the cabin I said, "Everything's old in here—bed frame, dresser, TV, pictures on the wall. Everything except the mattress. That's new, brand new."

"So what?" Maxe said. "Mattresses wear out."

"That's not the case here. Bartholomew replaced the old one because of bloodstains and bullet holes."

"Just guessing. Ain't you?"

"There's something else that isn't a guess," I said. "That picture of Christ over the bed...why was it hung off-center like that, down so low?" I went over and took the picture down. It had been screwed to the wall but I'd removed the screws earlier. "That's why."

Maxe stared at the hole in the wall—the little round hole that had been patched with wood putty but whose size and shape were still visible. The little round hole that had been made by a .32 caliber bullet. I stared at it too, as I had at four a.m. and with the same thought in my mind: I'd spent three nights in this damn room, on the same bed if on a different mattress. The thought started my skin crawling again; I shook it out of my mind. Dwell on a thing like that too long and it can make you a little crazy.

I said, "He'd have dug the slug out before he patched it. But the hole itself is enough. Added to the other evidence, it's enough."

Maxe's face was creased up like a hound's. "Just come over here in the night and blew them kids away?" he said with the same kind of awe I'd felt inside the Bartholomews' bedroom. "Just like that?"

"No, I don't think so. Something must have triggered the shooting—I doubt if it was premeditated."

"And afterward? What'd Ed do with the bodies?"

"Took them away somewhere. Buried or hid them. He'll tell the authorities where eventually. Or she will."

There was the sound of a car in the courtyard, crunching through the wet gravel. Maxe turned into the open doorway. Past him I could see the old Buick splash over to the rear of the office building, come to a stop. When Ed Bartholomew got out and started around to the passenger side, Maxe moved again in his jerky way—normal stride for a few paces, then a fast walk until he was almost running. I called, "Maxe, wait," but he didn't listen and didn't stop. All I could do then was to chase after him.

Both Bartholomews were out of the car, standing on the passenger side, him with his hand on his wife's arm, when Maxe reached them. They looked at him, at me coming up behind, at him again. There was nothing in Ed Bartholomew's eyes, no emotion, just a flat stare. If he was a closed book, Ruth Bartholomew was a wide open one with a cracked binding: unsteady on her feet, cheeks so pale the rouge on them was like daubs of crimson paint, eyes ablaze when they rested on me. She'd left all her love at the church. Now that she was home again, with her need for gin clawing at her, she had redonned her hate like a grotesque mask.

Bartholomew said, "What you doing here with that rifle, Art? And with *him?*" as I came up alongside Maxe. "What's going on?"

Maxe glanced at the rifle as if he'd forgotten he was carrying it. I thought he might blurt out the fact that I'd been inside their living quarters but he didn't. Nodding at me, he said, "He thinks you done something to them two kids last week. *Killed* them, for Chrissake, over there in Cabin Eleven."

It came out slap-hard, but neither of the Bartholomews reacted to it. There was not even a flicker of change in Ed Bartholomew's stoic expression. His wife's eyes seemed to get hotter, brighter—that was all. Neither of them said anything. The silence among the four of us was chill and dead, like night hush in a crypt.

"Well, Ed?" Maxe said at length. "You got anything to say?"

Bartholomew said, "No, I ain't," and turned and tried to prod his wife into walking away with him. She resisted. She had something to say.

"What's the matter with you, Art Maxe?" she demanded. Shrill-voiced, like a harpy. "You turning against your own kind? You're one of us, you're a God-fearing white man. He's an outsider and a nigger-lover. What in the Lord's name is wrong with you?"

Maxe didn't answer. Bartholomew pushed the woman this time, using his body, and got her swung around and moving toward their ugly little home. But she wasn't done talking yet. She called out over her shoulder, "Don't you listen to him. You're one of us, don't you ever forget that. We're kinsmen, Art Maxe—we're kinsmen!"

They were at the door by then; and a few seconds later they were gone inside.

"We ain't kinsmen," Maxe said to me. Then he said, "You were right. They done it."

21.

I left Maxe to do guard duty and went to make three calls on the public phone at the general store: the Modoc county sheriff's office, Joe DeFalco, and the FBI's district office in San Francisco. Then I returned to the Northern Comfort and waited with Maxe for the sheriff and his deputies to show up. The Bartholomews didn't try to run. Nor did they arm or barricade themselves inside. They didn't do anything. I would have been surprised if they had. It was one thing to take up weapons against what you believed was a coming race war; it was another thing to take up weapons against White Authority. Particularly when in your warped way of thinking, you hadn't really done anything wrong.

In a sense that was the most terrible fact of all. They truly did not believe they'd done anything wrong.

They made their confessions to the sheriff at twelve-fifteen that afternoon. I wasn't there when they opened up under questioning; Maxe and I were back at his garage, waiting there. One of the deputies came and told us. But I did get to see the transcriptions of their statements later on, and each one made me glad I hadn't been present to see and hear the words come out of their mouths.

Ruth Bartholomew: *They were making noise over in Eleven, laughing and whooping, just having themselves a gay old time. Wasn't nobody else staying with us that night so you could hear them plain. I went on over to see what they was up to. A body has to be careful in the motel business. Sometimes guests get rowdy, break things, you got to watch them like a hawk. The shade was up part way and the curtains was wide open, they didn't even have the decency to pull the shade or close the curtains, and there they were inside for all the world to see, naked as the day they was born, laughing and whooping and rolling around on the bed, him with his big black member sticking straight up in the air. Well, I was never so shocked in all my life. Never seen nothing so filthy lewd. White girl and that big buck nigger…we never even knew she was with a nigger. Ed never seen him when they checked in and neither did I, not until I looked in that window and seen him in there with her, kissing and playing with each other on one of my beds, practically right in my very own house. Well, it just made me crazy. Make any decent white person crazy. I don't remember getting the gun. Next thing I knew I had it in my hand and I was opening the door with my key and walking in there. I don't remember shooting her. Him, though, I remember kill-ing* him. *Two shots, one right in the middle of his black face. Nigger blood everywhere. Oh I remember that, all right. I'll never forget that. Sorry? No, I ain't sorry. Why should I be sorry? What they was doing, that coon and his white whore, they was sinning against the whole white race, against God Himself. They de-served to die … I was God's own instrument, sent to smite them down. I'd do it again the*

*same way if God give me the chance. You hear
me? I'd do it again the same way!*

Ed Bartholomew: *They was already dead,
both of them, when I come in. Wasn't much for
me to do except clean up the mess. I wrapped
them up in blankets and put them in the car.
Mattress and sheets too on account of all the
blood. Hurt my back doing all that heavy lift-
ing, my back ain't been the same since. Then
I took them out in the woods and dug a grave
and buried them. No, not too far, just a couple of miles over east. Next day I got their car
from Art Maxe and put their belongings in it
and drove over to Eureka and left it there and
come back on the bus. I guess that's all. I ain't
sorry it happened neither. Like Ruth said, it's
God's judgment. I don't see nothing to be sorry
for.*

Bartholomew took the sheriff and two
deputies to where he'd buried the bodies.
I wasn't there for that either; there was no
way I would have gone along even if I'd
been allowed to. Before they left I got permission from the sheriff to quit Creekside
for a while. Later on there was going to be

quite a party: DeFalco had said he would get a photographer and hire a plane and be up here in four or five hours. The FBI was also on the way; I'd laid the whole thing out for the agent in charge, with full details on the Kinsmen and their camp and the possible presence of Colonel Benjamin Darnell, fugitive. But I had time before any of them arrived, and I did not want to make my other two calls from this ugly little town with its ugly little people. They were no kinsmen of mine, either—none of them, not even Lena and Mike Cermak and Art Maxe.

I drove to Susanville and took a room in a Best Western I'd spotted yesterday. And then I made my last two calls, the hard ones, the ones I'd been dreading all day. One to Marian Shay and one to Rob Compton's parents, to tell them of the evil, intolerable thing that had been done to their children.

It's a hell of a world we live in. A hell of a world.